THE GODS IN WINTER

THE GODS IN WINTER
Patricia Miles

First Front Street paperback edtion, 2005

First published in the U.S. 1978 by E.P. Dutton

LIBRARY OF CONGRESS CATALOGING-IN-PUBLICATION DATA
Miles, Patricia.
The gods in winter / by Patricia Miles. – 1st Front Street pbk. ed.
p. cm.
Summary: When the Bramble family moves to a new home on the
grounds of an estate in Derbyshire, England, they hire a woman for home
help and become convinced that she is from a different time and place.
ISBN 1-932425-47-0 (pbk.: alk. paper)
1. Demeter (Greek deity)–Juvenile fiction.
[1. Demeter (Greek deity)–Fiction. 2. Moving, Household–Fiction.
3. Brothers and sisters–Fiction. 4. Mythology, Greek–Fiction.
5. Derbyshire (England)–Fiction. 6. England–Fiction.] I. Title.
PZ7.M5948Go 2005
[Fic]–dc22   2005012679
LCCN: 2005012679

FRONT STREET
An Imprint of Boyds Mills Press, Inc.
A Highlights Company

To my friend
Mary Woelfel Poole
with love

THE GODS IN WINTER

1

WE HAVE JUST had a family conference, Mum, Dad, Zach, Lottie and me—my name's Adam: Adam Bramble—and we have all agreed to say nothing, but nothing, about what has been happening here over the last few months. For three reasons: one, the danger is past, it seems. Two: *They* might not like it. And three: no one would believe us anyway—I shudder to think what my Aunt Cecilia (she's a child psychiatrist) would make of it, and Dad says he'd never hold up his head again as a serious scientist if any of it got out. So there it is, we are keeping silent out of a mixture of prudence and fear, not very noble qualities. But then, wait till you see what, or rather Who, we were up against.

Why the written account then, you might well ask: and who is going to read it?

Well, we've had rather a good idea about that, but first I'd like to explain why it's me who's doing the writing, and not for instance my mother, who after all had a degree in English from some posh college in the United States; or my Dad who's a physicist and always having to write reports on his research. It's all because of something my Dad read in a newspaper. Some Chief Inspector of Police had written in about children making the best witnesses. He said that adults often start changing things without meaning to, just to be helpful, but children don't know enough to guess what the police want. Apparently boys of nine or ten are absolutely the most accurate: they just say what they see. Well, I'm twelve, but Dad says I'll have to do, and so I've got the job. (Dad's going to look over it afterwards and suggest improvements: knowing my family, I expect they all will.)

Sometimes I shall have to ask other people about the things that happened to them—even, I suppose, my horrible cousin Crispin —but the beginning is easy. I can write that without any help.

Who am I writing it for? Well, for you, dear reader-in-the-future. You see, we can't quite pretend it never happened: we just don't want anyone to know about it while we're still around, that's all. This document is going to be buried in a place I know, and one day you'll find it, I hope. (I think there's some stuff buried under the Post Office Tower in London for someone to discover in the future—I just mention that, so you-in-the-future can find that too, if it's not been found already. You might get quite famous for finding things.)

Anyway, as I was saying—I'd have liked to put the whole thing on tape, really, and talked to you—you could have heard what I sound like, and it would have been more friendly—only Dad says it would have come a bit expensive, burying a tape-recorder as well as tapes I mean, as you, whoever you are in the future, might not have such things in your time. It's a pity, because English might even be a dead language by the time you get to read this, and you'd find out how to pronounce it. Anyway, I suppose I'll have to write it, but I'll make it as much like me talking to you as I can.

I'll begin with us setting out from Kent for our new home in the Midlands, because that's how it all started, on a fine October day last autumn ... There we are, the Bramble family—mother, father, three children and another little Bramble on the way—all bowling along northwards from London in a big old-fashioned car we've had since before I was born (1929 Daimler, as it happens, not vintage, just old). Our family was supposed to be complete with three children—hence Zach's initial and mine. A through Zee, as the Americans say—did I tell you my mother was an American?—only now there was going to be one more of us, and pretty soon at that. He or she would just be in time to get born in the new place. So—our old home was sold, all Dad's laboratory equipment had been moved, and we children had said goodbye to our respective schools (in Lottie's case not just the school, but goodbye desk, goodbye climbing frame, goodbye class Two bookshelf, etc. etc.—she's nine.)

The day was unusually warm for October—clear blue sky, the air like champagne, and we were in high spirits, gawping out of the windows with curiosity as the countryside whirled by, all very green and pretty in the sparkling sunshine. It came as quite a surprise to us.

"Where's all the coal mines and the factories, then?" I said.

"And where are all the dark Satanic mills?" inquired my mother.

"And what's happened to the Midlands?" said my Dad. "Aren't they supposed to be 'sodden and unkind'?"

My parents have an irritating habit of swapping quotations with each other. They do it partly to show that when they went to school people got a proper education with Greek and Latin and a lot of English poetry, not like us poor modern kids. It's funny, though Mum grew up in Massachusetts and Dad in Yorkshire they learned a lot of the same old poems and saw *all* the same old films. They usually stop reciting after a line or two, and it's my belief that's all they can remember. Anyway, while they were busy enjoying themselves in this highbrow way, we took the opportunity in the back seat to munch our way through a bag of sweets, though Lottie isn't supposed to eat many biscuits and sweets because of her teeth.

That reminds me that I forgot to tell you what we look like. There's no point in describing myself as I look absolutely normal —brown hair, brown eyes, if you want to know—but I've got a good description of Lottie and Zach for you, though it's not my own. My brother and sister used to go to one of these Junior Schools where they have the children's work, however awful, stuck up around the walls. On this particular day—which was, incidentally, the day we first heard we were moving—I had gone in to the top infants to collect Zach and this is what I saw fixed to his classroom wall for all to read, those who could read, that is.

My frend, by Gregory Dawson

(I'd heard evil things of this Gregory Dawson from Lottie, so I approached with interest.) It went something like this:

"My frend has mad blue eyes and neely white hair what stick up. He has a gruff voyce. Sometimes he act mad but he is all rite. He is neely 7."

So far so good—and my brother Zachary to the life. Unfortunately the writer then went on:

"is sister is like a stik inseck—" then, in case the reader hadn't quite got the point—

"she has arms and legs like stiks. She looks funy."

Lottie isn't all that peculiar, though I suppose she does look a bit like a pressed flower. Her face is sort of squashed thin like the rest of her, so there isn't quite room for her teeth and she has to wear a brace to push them flat. Also her nose sticks out a bit. You wouldn't think a kid her age would mind about her appearance but she does. My mother says she's going to be very beautiful when she grows up, like Dad's sister, our Aunt Cecilia: she was just the same as a child, said Mum, judging by some old photograph, since unfortunately lost. Lottie, not having seen the photograph, wasn't convinced. (This Aunt Cecilia is the one who's a child psychiatrist. More of her and her darling son Crispin later—drat, curse, etc.)

I rated one line of G. Dawson's dossier:

"is bruvver is a propa clever dik and a bigead"

I suppose the teacher thought no one would know who he meant, but they might just as well have labeled it: the Bramble family. It was us all right. Not a full stop in sight, but accurate. Near to it some other kid had drawn his mother and father looking like turnip heads and bawling each other out. Sometimes I think teachers are mad.

I stretched out my hand to rip G. Dawson's work from its moorings, when a voice of protest sounded at about the level of my elbow.

"Hey!"

I turned a beady eye upon the speaker and he dried up.

I don't normally go around treading on little kids' toes, but if I ever do, G. Dawson's will be the first.

"Are you Gregory Dawson? You were saying?"

"You leave that alone."

"Would you like to have your face pushed in?" I enquired pleasantly. Then I took the sheet down and stuck it in my pocket. Just in time, because a moment later Lottie came in from the school coach with her hair, which is brown and straight, all dripping wet from swimming. I'd forgotten it was her class's turn at the public swimming bath.

As it happened, she was already hopping mad about something but she kept it bottled up till we got home. Then she started storming around the house shouting "It's not fair! Why don't I ever get the nice things!" etc., etc.

You know how some things get you down? For instance, I get fed up with being the oldest one and having to be sensible all the time. I'm not sure what gets Zach down: he mostly lives in a happy little world of his own, but with Lottie it's the fact that everything improves *after* she's left and just in time for Zachary to enjoy it. For example, just after she'd gone up into the Juniors the Infants got a color TV set, and now she was nearly up to leaving the Juniors they were going to build a school swimming pool.

"... And Mum," she complained—at the top of her voice—"it'll probably take a whole year to build, and then I'll have left."

But it turned out that this time, for once, Lottie was wrong. Neither she nor Zach was going to be around to enjoy the new pool at St. Michael's Junior.

"Gather round, children," said our mother. "Time for me to spill the beans, I guess. We're moving."

Moving?!! Apparently my parents had known it might happen for ages, but they hadn't wanted to say anything until they were sure.

"So you calm down, Lottie Little," continued Mum. "We'll all be far from here long before the swimming pool's built. And—you just might have a lake of your own to swim in."

"What?"

"What did you say?"

"A *lake?*"

"*Of our own?*"—amazement all round.

Mum showed us a photograph of our new house. Did I say house?

"Crumbs, what is it?" squeaked Lottie.

"Oh, it's just a little old stately home of England that nobody wants," said Mum airily. "Don't snatch. You can look at it without holding it. It's supposed to be a copy of some place that used to belong to the Czar. You know, the Czar of all the Russias?" We nodded dumbly. "It's modeled on the Winter Palace in St. Petersburg, so I believe, the one Peter the Great built."

"Mon Dew," said Lottie, getting her breath back first. (She got

Mon Dieu from my French pen-friend who stayed with us, also *sapristi, parbleu*, and some worse things.)

"Will it be like St. Pancras Station in London?" she said.

"That's just a copy of the Czar's stables, nit," I told her, "not his palace."

"Huh." Lottie got her hands on the photograph. "It doesn't look a bit Russian, more sort of Greek with those pillars and triangle bits."

"That's right," said Mum approvingly. "It's in the classical style. That means the Russians copied it from the Greeks."

"Oh," said Lottie, looking at the photograph. "Then this is a copy of a copy."

"Yes—like those pictures you used to get on Marmite jars," I said intelligently. But Mum groaned, and told us to stop it, and Zach, who was losing the thread, very sensibly asked:

"Where is this place?"

"It's in Derbyshire—in the north somewhere," said Mum, waving a hand vaguely in the air. She's not too strong on English geography.

"It's in the Midlands," I said.

"Oh," said Zach. "I thought it was in Russia."

"No, Zach," I explained, with elder-brother-type patience. "You're not going to live in Russia, Greece, and you're not going to live in a railway station. You're going to a big house, about 150 miles north of here, where we live now, in Kent."

"Oh." He seemed satisfied.

"I'm afraid we're not exactly living in the stately home," said Mum. "That's just where Dad's office will be, and they're going to build labs out at the back and so forth, but the Ministry's taken over the whole estate and we'll have a little house in the grounds somewhere.

"Oh. But there is a lake?" said Lottie anxiously.

"Oh yes, there's a lake, and gardens and waterfalls, and the whole place is set on the edge of wild moors."

"Cor. When are we going?"—this from me.

"In a couple of months," Mum said. "You can finish out the term where you are, then we'll get ourselves ready."

And that's what we had done, and I'd better get back to our journey, only shall I just tell you, for the sake of completeness, what our parents are like? I'll keep it short. Well, in a way they're sort of opposite. For instance, Mum likes company, but Dad likes it when there's just us. Dad's lean and dark, and mostly thinking of something else. What I mean is, when you ask him things, he looks at you without speaking, then he sort of blinks and says "Oh—er—" before he replies, as if the question has a lot of brain to get through. He does give you the answer: sometimes he tells you more than you want to know—have you noticed that with teachers and such like? He works in a Government Science Research Institute —on aspects of mining. That's how he describes himself. He says "aspects" is a good word, it can mean anything. My mother has tons of energy and is always on the ball. She's blonde and rather hefty and very emancipated and all that.

I suppose that's why she was insisting now on having a turn of driving—despite expecting the baby—a short turn anyway, once we got off the motorway. As we drove on the ground began to get a bit hillier.

Pretty soon we were watching out for our exit. "It's not far now," said Dad. "Do you see the moors beginning to rise up ahead—that sort of purplish line in the distance?"

"Not long now till the exciting bit," said Mum.

Prophetic words!

Then we left the motorway, went round a roundabout, and found ourselves after a few hundred yards in a very countrified little lane. Dad stopped the car and they swapped over.

Quite close to us a girl was climbing a fence into a field of cut corn. She had black silken hair and round her neck a scarf, bright red, like a poppy. I suppose I thought that because the field happened to be full of poppies. Beyond them there was a sheet of water and a little wood. The whole scene looked like a picture in a Beginner Reading book: yellow stubble, red flowers, blue water—all of it strangely clear and bright—and in the foreground, the dark-haired girl. As we passed her, she looked up at us and smiled. We smiled back.

"What a marvelous looking girl," said my mother. "*She's* got straight hair." She never misses a chance of cheering Lottie up.

As we reached the next bend I looked back. The girl was starting to pick the poppies.

"She's not supposed to pick the flowers, is she?" said Zach.

"Can I pick some?" said Lottie.

"No; we're not stopping," said Dad.

"They don't last anyway, honey." Mum drove on. Then— "Strange, that," she said. "They're awfully late, aren't they?"

"What are?" asked Dad.

"Those poppies."

"No they're not. You often get a second lot at the end of the summer."

"This late? Rubbish—if you ask me something very odd is happening to our climate."

"No it isn't."

They can keep up a verbal tennis match like this for miles: in the back seat Lottie gave me a nudge and grinned. "Watch this." She shaped the words silently, then said aloud: "Er—Dad? Can I have a biscuit? One of those chocolate chip cookies?"

Dad passed us the whole packet, without either of them noticing. (Pop-eyed grin here from Zach, and other silent expressions of glee on the back seat.)

"Truly," my mother was saying, "this is Mediterranean weather."

"No, not really. It's not all that hot."

"Well, it's not natural to England. I mean, this is *England*—where's the rain?"

Dad said: "It's not all that unnatural. It's just different from what we've had for the last few hundred years. Weather moves in belts. You get wet spells and dry ones. It's quite normal to have changes over long periods. For instance, all that Greek civilization stuff would probably never have happened if they hadn't had about five hundred years of more northerly weather. In fact, this is very much the kind of weather they had then."

(I have to tell you, my parents are the type who sit listening to quiz shows and know all the answers. When he retires my Dad is going to write a book called "Funny Things Not Many People Know.")

"Seriously," he went on "Greece *was* probably very like this in classical times."

"Oh, and I suppose that would put Mount Olympus somewhere in the Peak District. Ho ho!" scoffed my mother, looking round alarmingly at the rest of us for support.

It was perhaps curious that at this moment we saw the temple. At least, for a minute we thought it was a temple.

"What's that thing?" demanded Zach, staring. Actually, it was only a rather grand entrance to a cemetery, with pillars and a domed roof: when we looked we could see an ordinary old gray village church beyond it.

"Ah," said Dad. "We're nearer than I thought. Look out for a crossroads."

Mum drove past the cemetery and in a little while reached the crossroads. There was no signpost, and on our map there was a name printed right across the bit we wanted: Blodgett Hall, it said. That was the proper name of the place we were looking for, Blodgett Hall Estate—though we'd been calling it the Winter Palace. Dad pored over the map for a bit and then said "Turn left."

"Are you sure?"

"Yes."

The road, which was narrow enough before, deteriorated into an even smaller country lane, heavily shaded by trees.

Mum said "This has got to be the wrong road: it's too narrow."

"Just you carry on," said Dad in a calm reassuring voice. Actually I could see his face in the driving mirror and I could tell from his expression he wasn't all that sure. She drove on a bit farther, with the hedges closing in on us all the time.

"See—what did I tell you. Look at that thing up ahead under the trees. It's a danger sign. Pretty soon there's going to be no road at all."

"What's there a danger of?" asked Zach, with his mouth full of biscuit. You'd laugh if you could hear him. He has a great big deep voice you would think was coming out of somebody twice his size.

"I'll stop the car and you can read it," said Mum, who is very keen on us using our own brains. Zach made a horrible face behind her back, then he slogged his way through the notice. What it said was:

DANGER. ROAD LIABLE TO SUBSIDENCE.

He was no wiser. "What does that mean?"

"It just means we're over the coalfield," said Dad. "Sometimes the old tunnels give way underground; then the road's liable to cave in."

"What's 'liable to'?" asked Lottie.

"Can't you guess?" said my mother.

"Does it mean 'it might happen'?"

"Yes," said Dad, "only it probably won't. It's nothing to bother about. You see signs like that all over the Midlands."

"Great," said Mum. "What kind of a place is this you're bringing us to? The climate's changed and the ground's liable to give way … Brr! I'm not too sure about the climate. It's colder under these trees."

"Are you all right? Would you like me to drive again?" said Dad.

"Would you mind, honey?"

"I don't mind. Are you sure you feel all right?"

"I'm fine—a bit uncomfortable with the baby." Mum laughed. "I guess I'm just not in much shape to do emergency stops if the ground gives way. I'll read the map, and maybe we'll get somewhere."

They swapped over again, and we changed round too. It was Lottie's turn to be in the middle. She decided to kneel up and look out of the back window. We drove out of the shade and into the sunshine again, but we hadn't got very far when:

"Look!" yelled Lottie. "The ground's shifting. I saw it move."

My father slammed on the brakes and got out. He stood looking back down the road shielding his eyes.

"Noodle," he said. "It's heat haze off the road."

"You've come too far past it," said Lottie feebly. "It was back round that bend where I saw it."

"Rubbish." He had just opened the door to get in again when a huge black open car, all glistening and gleaming—vintage, not old —shot round the corner from behind. The brakes shrieked, the tires squealed, and our Dad leapt for his life. Two wheels went up on the bank and the car tilted towards us. For a terrifying moment two tons of steel overshadowed us, blotting out the sky. Then it lurched past. The driver kept an arm like a vice around his passenger—a girl. She screamed with fright as they bucketed down on to the surface and disappeared at speed up the lane ahead. Bracken and meadowsweet trailed from the fender.

We were a little while getting ourselves back together again. Then Mum drew a long shuddering breath and Lottie broke the spell: "What a horrible man! I hate him!" She was staring at the road. I looked down and saw what she meant.

"There are now two sparrows fewer in the world," I said.

"You were nearly one father short, never mind sparrows," said our Dad with feeling. Mum was still gazing after the car.

"Coming from nowhere like that," she said. "He could have killed us all. Ugh. I've gone cold all over."

"I don't know why you ever said it was hot," complained Lottie. "I'm freezing. I've gone all shivery right up my neck."

"That girl who was with him," said Mum "—she screamed."

"You'd scream if I drove like that. He only had one hand on the wheel. Who does he think he is—King of the Road?"

"You must admit, he'd got the car for it, Dad," I said.

Mum went on puzzling it over. "… I wonder. Do you know, I think he'd only just picked her up. Wasn't she the one we saw back there in the field? I'm sure I saw a flash of scarlet silk."

Dad shrugged. "I didn't see: I was too busy saving my neck." He started the engine again. Mum lowered her voice: "I just hope she knows what she's doing, that's all."

In the back seat Lottie piped up virtuously, "You shouldn't accept lifts from strange men." After that the subject was dropped.

We pushed on. We were all beginning to get a bit tired by now but we weren't through yet. It did seem to have got darker and colder. A bank of cloud crept up over the sun and the sky went sort of grayish-white all over. Ahead the lane seemed to go on for ever. At last Mum said, "This is what I call typical English weather: it's not raining, it's not cold, it's not hot, it's not anything. Even the sky's the color of nothing."

"I feel cold," said Zach.

"I'll close the windscreen," said Dad. (You can have it open on our car, it's that old.) He was just winding it shut with one hand as he drove along, when "Watch out!"—I don't know which one of us called out, I think two people did at once, and Zach was saying "What's all that dust?", and Mum was shrieking "Stop! Stop!" and we juddered to a halt on the edge of a great gaping hole that stretched right across the road and into the fields on either side as well, and I don't know how many yards long. The hedge had gone, and the dust was still rising out of it. Like lightning Dad backed the car a good long way before any of us uttered a word.

"Holy cow!" Dad said at last. "It's that idiot's fault, tearing along like a maniac. The road must have caved in behind him."

Mum said, "You don't suppose … They couldn't have fallen in, could they?"

"I'll take a look."

"Don't!"

"Can we come?"

"No!"

Dad walked cautiously towards the hole, and none of us said a word till he got back. Mum gave us a sweet while we waited. Mum ate her sweet with the paper on.

He came back quite quickly. "I'll inform the police. They'll have to close the road. It's a frightful hole—an absolute chasm—but I think if they'd had an accident I would have seen some sign of it …"

"It seems incredible," said Mum, "that you could just get swallowed up, driving along in little safe old England."

Dad turned the car in a gateway and we got going back out of the lane, and pretty well held our breath till we reached the crossroads again.

"Well," said Mum, "more betterer we try the other way, I guess."

("More betterer" is one of Zach's expressions which has passed into the family language, though he doesn't say it himself anymore.)

This time we went straight on through a little village—just a handful of stone cottages—and finally the road brought us to a gatehouse, another Greek-looking thing, with a long, long drive winding away beyond the gates into the distance. There was a notice which said:

Ministry of Fuel and Power. Keep Out

A man in uniform let us in and gave Dad a map of the grounds. Dad asked him to ring the police right away about the subsidence. The man said he would, then saluted, closed the gates behind us, and went into his little house. "Did you tell him about the car and the girl?" said Mum. Dad nodded. We drove on.

"*Parbleu*," said Lottie. "Imagine owning so much land that you even have your own roads."

"Hey! They've got their own speed limit," said Zach. "Fifteen miles an hour."

"Don't say 'Hey'," said Mum automatically.

Then we all dried up as we swept round a big lawn and came opposite the main building—a house so huge, heavy and repellent that for a moment it robbed us all of words—no mean feat in our family.

"Perhaps it looked better when it was new," said my father faintly.

"It sure looked a whole lot better in the photographs," said my mother. "I didn't know it was going to be made of *concrete*."

It stood on rising ground, four-square, massive, and socked you in the eyeballs. Behind it the moor rose, grim and wild, except for one great spread of dark green—gardens maybe—that covered the slope behind the house.

"I believe the Coal Board got it cheap," said Dad.

"I'm not surprised."

"It's been empty a long time."

I said "There's just one word to describe it—*horrible!*"

And that about summed up the family's point of view, except for Zach. He said admiringly, "It's big, isn't it?" Then "I like it"—he's often the odd one out.

"Drive on, "said Mum grimly.

On we drove, in a stunned silence, through the rolling parkland. After that, our house, when we reached it, wasn't just a pleasant surprise, it was a real relief. It was just an old stone farmhouse that had got swallowed up by the estate—Birch Tree Farm, our new home. My parents turned to each other with a soppy look on their faces.

"It's not unlike the cottage we saw at …"

"Just what I was thinking."

The long journey, the maniac in the sports car, the hole in the ground, faded from our minds.

"Good heavens," said Mum, "look at all the outbuildings."

We tumbled out of the car, and glad to do it.

"Stables!" shrieked Lottie. She started tossing her head and pawing the ground, or whatever horses do, and pranced off round the corner of the house. She spends a good bit of her time, mentally, pacing about on a milk-white steed. It was all out of books—she'd only been on a horse about twice in her life.

"Hey!" said Zach. "That lake. It's here— right by our house."

There it was, at the bottom of a slope beyond our new front garden. Zach was looking at it longingly, only he knew he wouldn't be allowed to swim, as he'd just got over a bout of earache.

Dad said "Never mind, old son: it's probably colder than it looks."

I was counting the windows on the farmhouse. I was wishing and hoping I could have a room of my own. It looked as if it might be possible. Dad opened the gate. A tall birch tree with little gold leaves stood by it. I followed him up a flagged path, with a lawn and bushes on either side.

"What's that red thing stuck on your shoe, Dad? There—caught in the buckle."

"Oh, that. Scuffed it up on the road somewhere I suppose." He pulled at it and it came apart in his fingers: a short hairy stalk and the head of a flower. It was a dead poppy.

2

WE HADN'T BEEN in our new home more than two or three days when Dad had to go away to an engineering conference. He's always going off to things like that, sometimes abroad—this time it was Finland—and Mum never likes it. In fact, she'd been liking it less and less as the time got nearer for the new baby to arrive. Zach, Lottie and I don't like it much either. He used to bring us smashing presents home, only lately that had all gone a bit wrong. We'd got so that we always expected things, but he didn't always have the time now to shop, or sometimes he just forgot. I wouldn't like you to think we're really greedy, but it's a funny thing—the presents did make it a whole lot better if he had gone on a trip.

Anyway, it was a Friday, about midday. We were due to start school the following Monday: we'd more or less spent the week helping to make the house cozy, and that was a good thing because the weather had changed, it had gone all wild and autumnal and more like October is supposed to be. Dad arrived home. He came striding in at the kitchen door with a big friendly grin on his face —and found Mum, Lottie and me all lined up with expectant looks on our faces. Zach was off playing by himself somewhere. The thing I was hoping for was a knife—one of those strong-bladed

PATRICIA MILES

ones with a handle made of reindeer hoof—Mum wanted something for the house, and Lottie had asked him to bring her anything red to wear from Lapland. He remembered as soon as he saw us, and we could tell from his face we were out of luck. There were hellos all round, and it was a minute or two till the storm burst.

"I'm glad you got back safely—even if you did forget us," said Mum eventually.

"I'm sorry I didn't bring you anything—I just didn't have time."

At once Lottie and I started behaving horribly. We acted all pathetic and hurt and not able to speak. Mum stopped smiling. She didn't say anything either.

"For Heavens' sake," said Dad. "Why can't you get it into your heads? I've not been on holiday. I don't *choose* to go. I go to *work*."

No response.

"You never said you wanted anything … er … did you?"

Silence.

Then a great whoosh of wind slammed the door back on its hinges and sent dust and dead leaves whirling in round our legs. It seemed to spark Dad into a rage.

"Well, say something, somebody!"

"Could you close the door," said Mum, in a sort of icy, polite way "—because of the wind? I'd just swept the floor before you came in."

Lottie and I held our breath. Dad paused for a moment, then changed his tack.

"What you want," he said soothingly, "is a nice cup of …"

Don't say it, Dad! I thought.

"… tea."

On the word "tea" our mother went up like a rocket.

"Tea!" she yelled. "I might have known! The British answer to everything. It's sympathy I want, consideration, a little human kindness."

"… and a present," said Dad.

Oh brother! By chance there was a nearly full pot of lukewarm tea standing on the table. I'd made it myself some time before. My mother's glance lit on it and her hand shot out. Her eyes positively flashed: she seemed to have gone all elemental, like the weather.

"Diademia!" Dad put out a hand. (That's my Mum's name: Diademia Scarlett Bramble.)

She's going to throw it, I thought, she's really going to throw it. And she did. Only not at my father. She smashed it down hard on the kitchen floor, and it sort of exploded. Bits of pot leapt up into the air and a fine dew of tea clung to everything, including my mother's hair. As if that wasn't enough, she picked up the sugar bowl (full), and slammed that down too. Some of the crystals clung to her hair, now damp from the tea. She looked like a demented sugar-frosted rice crispy. Never, never in the history of the family before had anything happened like this.

All of a sudden the wind dropped. There was a moment of absolute stillness. A very strange electric moment—while Dad, Lottie and I stood gawping at her in an awestruck way. We all stood frozen like a scene at a waxworks, Mum as well, and in the silence we heard the door-bell ring on the far side of the house. Lottie and I risked breathing again, and a few seconds later Zach came sunnily into the room.

"Hey! The home help's come. Oh hello, Dad!"

"If ever a home needed help …" I couldn't resist saying that.

Mum glared at me. "Don't you start being funny." As if I would.

"What home help?" said my father.

"We're going to have a family retainer," said Zach—that's what Lottie and I had told him, just to make it more interesting.

"Best thing since sliced bread," said Lottie nervously. She'd heard that somewhere and kept on saying it till it drove us all mad.

"She's going to help me with the baby," said Mother, who was suddenly completely calm again, only calmer than ordinary calm, if you know what I mean—she's good at these dramatic switches.

"But you haven't got the baby yet," protested Dad.

"I daresay. But it's only a question of time." Mum turned to Zach, still all serene. "Has she brought her luggage with her?"

"What do you mean: has she brought her luggage with her?" Now Dad's face turned to thunder. "You're not going to tell me you've asked her to *live in, here, with us?*"

"You weren't here so I've made my own arrangements," said Mother loftily. "You'll be able to go abroad now just as the fit takes you, and you won't have to worry about us at all."

"Our last home help didn't live in," spluttered Dad. "She went home every night."

"I somehow got the feeling Mrs. Korngold has no home of her own to go to."

"Mrs. *Korngold?*" said Dad. "Is she a foreigner or something?"

"She might be—like me," said Mum crisply.

Poor Dad, I thought: shot down in flames again.

"Well, don't let's keep her standing on the doorstep," said Mum. "Go and let her in, Adam."

I hurried off. I was glad to get out of the kitchen.

I don't know what I expected when I went into the hall. An unusually large woman, dressed shabbily in black, was standing at the door—from the village, I supposed, and yet, I don't know why, I immediately had the impression that she'd come a much greater distance than that. Her face had a worn, overstrained look, and she carried a bulging black bag. She reminded me vaguely of something I'd once seen, some disaster … people in distress. All at once a picture came into my mind, very clear, like an old black and white newsreel from the war. There were families fleeing along the roads, pushing their possessions along in handcarts, prams, bicycles, anything. Then Stukas started dive-bombing and machine-gunning people—it came back to me: they were refugees.

That's what she had reminded me of: she was like a refugee.

Then the planes went away and some of the people got up and there was a woman crying …

It's not usual with me to see pictures that aren't there. I rubbed my hand across my face.

She was looking at me with a strange penetrating gleam in her eye—kind, but penetrating. She had the most amazing blue eyes.

I managed to blurt something out at last: "Are … are you the home help, please?"

Her expression changed. "Yes," she said, rather vaguely, "that's it—the home help."

She didn't sound foreign. She didn't sound anything in particular: perhaps a bit slow and countrified—but I'm not much good at spotting things like that.

"Come in," I said, and took her to my mother.

"Mrs. Korngold? You're very welcome." My mother greeted her in gracious tones.

Mrs. Korngold nodded and smiled—and if she thought there was something odd about my mother's hair, she didn't reveal it by so much as a flicker of an eyelid. Mum made a few swift introductions, and then said, "I'll show you to your room."

"Thank you. That will be very nice."

My father was led away by Lottie: he was muttering under his breath something cross about "decrepit old retainers."

The funny thing was when I went into the kitchen not very long after, decrepit or not, Mrs. Korngold had got it straight again, tea, sugar and all. She must have flashed around at the speed of light —it was really amazing, all neat and cozy and comfortable, and pretty soon marvelous smells began floating into the hall.

It must have been an hour later when the phone rang. Dad took the call. In a minute we could hear his raised voice: "What do you mean, you can't let us have a home help? We've already got the one you sent. Not one of yours? I suggest you try to run your department with more efficiency. Your right hand obviously doesn't know what your left hand's doing. Don't bother—we'll keep the one we've got." He slammed down the phone.

"That's funny," said Mum. "I filled in a form at the office, and later she just rang me up herself. Still, who cares, if it works out all right."

So Mrs. Korngold moved in. It was as simple as that. And she did suit us—or was it that we suited her?

At this point I'd better say a word about how we live. It's like this: my mother is all right on the absolutely basic stuff like: are the main living areas clean, is there food in the house, and are our school clothes fit to be seen? Actually the food can be quite good. But after that things tail off rather, e.g. my bedroom floor gets swept from time to time, especially if someone's coming. But if I want to have model airplanes all over my room (which I do), it's up to me if I want them encrusted with dust or not. Well, right from the start Mum and Mrs. Korngold hit it off to a T, so in fact we went on just the way we always have, except that with cries of glee Mum now got down to some stuff she's been working on for the Open University.

Where did Mrs. Korngold come from, if not from the Home Help Organization, or National Health or whatever? At the time none of us gave it much thought. As far as we were concerned we had plenty of other things to think about. Our new schools for instance. Lottie and Zach had a nice little village school to go to, but I wasn't much looking forward to mine.

My new school was a bike-ride away in the nearest town—an all-male public school which took a few day boys. (I used to go to a comprehensive school before.) It would have been nice if I'd had someone to go with. A few of the other scientists did have children, but they were nearly all either older or younger than us, and the odd one or two who were my age went away to boarding schools. On my way there that first day I kept thinking of a daft prayer Lottie's class had made up for the school leavers at St. Michael's Junior. It went something like this:

When we cannot find our way in the corridors of our new schools,
God help us.
When we cannot remember our new teacher's name,
God help us, etc. etc.

That expresses more or less how I felt.

The first day turned out not to be too bad until we got to the last two lessons of the afternoon. I had palled up with a boy called Rumbold, and I was sitting next to him. I had just asked him "What is big and hairy and flies round a candle flame?" (a hairy mam-moth, in case you'd like to know), when I noticed he wasn't listening at all. Instead he had his nose stuck in his briefcase, and he was muttering "Oh my God: I've forgotten my physics notebook! Oh my God, what shall I do?" Just out of sympathy a nerve started hopping on the back of my knee. It does that when I'm scared. I'd remembered then, we were due for a double period with Mr. Busby, who taught physics and chemistry, and of whom I already had heard tell. Rumor had it that he spent his spare time trying to turn base metal into gold, and if using the entrails of a couple of Form One boys would have helped in any way he wouldn't have hesitated.

In he strode. I don't know—people will exaggerate. I wouldn't have said he was more than six feet four and three feet broad, myself. Black hair, black bushy beard, and black horn-rimmed spectacles completed this picture. A silence as of the grave had fallen on the class, and I mentally added a line to Lottie's litany:

When we have double science, God help us.

Still, since caning is pretty well out of date now, I was wondering what else he could do to us, besides look the way he did. I didn't have to wonder for long. He was a specialist in the following: chalk-throwing, i.e. chalk flies at speed of bullet towards victim's head; desk-thumping, loud and sudden under victim's nose; the thousand-volt glare; the very loud voice, "WHAT do you think you're doing?"; etc. etc.

We took notes almost the whole time, and Rumbold used his French exercise book. Just when he thought he'd got away with it, right at the end of the double period, Mr. Busby came up to him. He knotted a brawny hand into Rumbold's shirt, vest, etc. and clamped him against the wall at his own eye level. Then he said, in a voice that started mildly, "You will copy out your work tonight into the proper notebook, Rumbold—your physical science notebook. I'll see it in the morning. You won't forget to bring it, WILL YOU?"

"N-no, sir."

He put him down quite gently and turned to me.

"Ah—new boy. Bramble, isn't it?"

"Yes sir!" I dare say his voice had quietened by ten decibels or so, but I got the message, viz. he ruled the world, and the sooner I cottoned the better.

I must say, I was glad to get home at the end of the day. We had a nice evening, though one slightly strange thing happened. It was only a little thing really. Mrs. Korngold had brought some coffee after supper into the sitting-room. "Oh! I forgot the milk," she said. The door shuddered to behind her, and we all heard her bounding along the passage to the kitchen with her long energetic stride.

"What a noisy woman," said Dad. "I can't make her out. She's very energetic for such an old lady."

"I don't think she's all that old," said my mother.

Dad said "How old *do* you think she is?"

"About my age," said Mum.

"No she isn't," he contradicted. "She's a lot older."

"She can't be all that much older—she's got a daughter who's not quite grown up," said Lottie.

"How do you know?"

"She told me."

"I think she's quite young," said Zach.

"Gosh," I said, "you'd think we were all seeing a different person."

"Well, anyway," said Dad, "she's certainly not much like that character we had before, when Lottie was born—Mrs. Slip Slop, or whatever she was called."

"Oh, that poor thing," said my mother, "she always had too much to do, with that ghastly family she had. I know what you mean, though."

"Why did you call her Mrs. Slip Slop?" asked Lottie—no doubt because it seemed vaguely to have something to do with that important event, her own arrival in the world.

"It was the way she walked," said Mother, "terrifically fast, but most peculiar—she wore down-at-heel slippers and never raised her heels off the ground, as if she hadn't the energy—sort of dry-land skiing."

The door opened, and in glided Mrs. Korngold with the milk. We hadn't heard her coming—point number one. Second point—she was shuffling along the carpet without raising her heels. *It was just as if she had plucked the image of Mrs. Slip Slop, the home help, straight out of my parents' minds:* and used it.

But I think the first real hint I got that there was definitely something strange about Mrs. Korngold came one Wednesday not long after I started school. As this school is a posh one it does posh things like calling homework "prep," and we get a half-holiday in the middle of the week (we have to go in on Saturday mornings instead). So, it was a Wednesday afternoon and I was at home.

Zach was at home too. His worst thing is that he's always getting earache. It's actually made him a bit deaf in one ear. Anyway, Mum let him go outside, well wrapped up—he was just getting over a bout—and went upstairs for a rest herself. Zach was quite happy running around the garden pretending to be an airplane, with his arms spread out. I was reading a book in Dad's study, when Mrs. Korngold came in and started dusting the piano in a casual sort of way—I used to learn the piano, but I've given it up, thank goodness. She stopped, and I just happened to look up and saw her staring at a picture we've got hanging between the piano and the bookcase—it's one of those writhing-about pictures of cornfields in the South of France, by Van Gogh, I think. Anyway, there's a cornfield in it and bushes and things.

"I like that," she said. "That pleases me." Carelessly she flicked her duster over the reproduction, and—this is the queer bit—*the corn in the picture moved.* It swayed. So did the bushes. That wasn't all. When I looked out of the window a moment later something very odd was happening in the garden too—*all the plants were writhing about.* I could see them slowly twisting, more or less *visibly growing.* There was a crab apple tree with a few leaves and apples still on, not swaying or anything, but sort of vibrating. It was using its strength to hold up its branches. Crikey, I thought, I'm seeing things. I didn't feel dizzy or anything. Nothing was moving fast, only pulsating. But I just had this impression of tremendous energy quietly fizzing away out there in the garden. It didn't look less real or blurred or anything. Just the opposite: it looked terribly alive.

I tottered back. Mrs. Korngold had come up behind me—she

had a habit of standing staring out of the window, and she was staring now—only she didn't seem a bit surprised. She had a kind of brooding, hooded look about the eyes, as if she'd forgotten where she was for a moment. Then she blinked, and when I looked back the garden was just the same as gardens always are. Mrs. Korngold shuffled off out into the hall—back to being Mrs. Slip Slop again.

A moment later she returned. "What's the word he's saying?"

"Who? Oh, Zach!"

I listened for a minute. He was still running round talking to himself, just repeating the same word: "Subsi.i.i.idence, subsi. idence."

"Subsidence?" I said. "It's when you get a sort of hole in the ground."

"I know that. Why is he saying it?"

"We saw one."

She seized hold of me by the wrist. "What? A hole? How big?"

"Dad had to go to the police about it. The road gave way when we were coming here and a man in a car nearly killed our Dad. He was driving like a maniac and he had a girl with him. Mrs. Korngold, you're hurting me. You're crushing my arm!"

She let go, and bit by bit I told her all that had happened on our journey to Blodgett Hall. She looked terrible when I'd finished.

She sort of reeled off to the kitchen. I followed her down the passage, wondering what on earth to do. Mum was still lying down resting and I didn't want to bother her. I didn't know what was up with Mrs. Korngold, but I thought perhaps I'd give her a drink— the strongest I could find. We had some stuff called ouzo—we'd had it for ages. Dad brought it back from a trip. It looks like milk, smells of aniseed and kicks like a mule. It's clear like gin, but when you add water it goes cloudy. Dad says if you don't add water, the top of your head flies off. I fixed Mrs. Korngold a drink, made it nice and cloudy, and crept softly away.

Her hand had closed round the glass, but when I looked back at her from the door she hadn't touched it. She was still sitting there two hours later when Lottie ran in from school. She looked up then: her face was all contorted with grief. Suddenly she cried out in an agonized voice: "She's gone. She's gone!"

It was terrible to watch. We'd got used to Mrs. Korngold being calm and strong. Dignified. It was like seeing a hillside break up.

She started groaning. "I knew it," she moaned, "I knew it all the time." Two big tears spilled over out of her eyes and rolled down her face.

"Oh, don't cry, Mrs. Korngold!" Lottie threw her arms round her. "What's wrong?

I just stood sheepishly by.

"It's my daughter," said Mrs. Korngold. "I miss my daughter, and I want her back!"

I pried the glass out of her fingers and made her a fresh drink. What do you think she did with it? She took it outside—we followed: across the yard, past the stables, and into the orchard. Then she tipped it up—I thought she was throwing it away—and sloshed some out, three times on to the ground. She drank the rest. Not that there was much left by then, fortunately, because as we were coming back towards the house Mum appeared at the kitchen door, with a kind of fluttery smile on her face.

"Battle stations, family," she said, "the baby's on its way at last. Adam, ring your father: tell him I've got the midwife, and the doctor, but he'll have to take you three over to the Pembertons. Lottie, put the kettle on. Mrs. Korngold, will you help me? Am I glad you're here!" She turned to go in.

Mrs. Korngold put her hand on my shoulder. Straightened up. Wiped her eyes. Steadied herself.

"Never fear: I'll come."

She walked stiffly into the house.

3

THESE PEMBERTONS we were going to while the baby was getting itself born were my Dad's boss and his wife—Sir Charles and Lady Pemberton. Sir Charles is the director of the whole research establishment. Their own family's grown up, but he and his wife are still quite fond of children. They have always been extremely nice to us, and it was great to be going there anyway, because they had just moved into a flat in the Winter Palace itself.

We hadn't seen the inside yet but Dad said it was a whole lot better than the outside, and that we would be truly amazed. Zach said he didn't know what we were going on about, and what was wrong with the outside? He still thought it was very nice—and big. He was right about that. Dad marched us in under a huge porch propped up on pillars, and knocked on a door about ten feet high— it took a grown man to lift the knocker. Then he shouted: "Open Sesame!"

The door swung open and we walked in. Lady Pemberton was waiting to welcome us. Dad handed us over, chatted for a couple of minutes, and pushed off.

Dad was right: it really was great inside. Where we came in at the entrance hall—a vast open space with a massive staircase rising out of it—there was this strange marble floor. It was patterned in blocks of black and white, in twists and curves, and after a minute we realized it was in the shape of a maze. To our left double doors, all white and gold, opened in to an oval-shaped ballroom. (Most of the other rooms were being turned into offices—there were workmen leaving when we arrived—but they were keeping the ballroom as it was, in case they wanted a big room for conferences.) Lady Pemberton took us into the ballroom and told us the floor was sprung for dancing. We took off our shoes and she let us jump up and down on it. Zach was disappointed—he thought it was going to be like a trampoline, which would have been pretty daft in a ballroom, as I pointed out, but you could feel it was a bit springy. And there were pictures painted on the actual walls. They looked like Roman stuff, only when you looked harder you could see it was all mines and factories and shipyards done in very pale colors, and unfortunately splodged with damp here and there.

It wasn't long before we had an uncomfortable feeling that someone was giving us a very cold look indeed. Fortunately it turned out to be only a portrait, but life-size and the only one in the room. It was of the man who had owned the estate, a tall formidable-looking man, shown standing by a roll-top desk. He wore an old-fashioned business suit—black jacket, striped trousers and a wing collar. His dark hair was streaked with iron gray. His name was William Blodgett and afterwards he was made a lord.

It was one of those pictures with eyes that follow you wherever you stand—chilly blue eyes, and his mouth was like a steel trap. One hand was curled lovingly round something on the top of the desk: it proved to be a bust of himself.

"Old devil," said Lady Pemberton, while we all gazed up at him. "Oh, I suppose he wasn't too bad really. He was just the complete autocrat. Everyone had to do what he said. He had a whole village shifted to make room for this place."

We had a few extra jumps on the floor. Finally Lottie stopped sliding around and asked Lady Pemberton: "Why doesn't Mr. Thing, I mean Earl Bloggs—you know—live here now?"

"He's dead. His son inherited it but he didn't want to live here."

"He must be barmy," said Zach. "I wouldn't mind living here. Hey, look at the ceiling."

"Don't say 'Hey'," said Lottie. But we did look. Crumbs, it was painted all over with the same pattern of a maze we had seen in the hall. In the space in the middle, where you expect to see something sort of important that the maze is leading to, it just showed a dark blue sky with stars and against it some twirly gold letters, a 'W' and a 'B' intertwined. William Blodgett's initials, held up by smiling cherubs. I burst out laughing.

"How daft."

"I think it's a nice idea," said Lottie.

"So do I," said Zach.

We came back through the hall and Lady Pemberton let us play about on the floor maze for a bit (it had a coat of arms in the middle). Then we went up the stairs, past huge mirrors, and Lottie said, "I wouldn't look in all these mirrors if I was here by myself —in case I wasn't there." She's always having good ideas like that. Zach said he betted that when you looked in it all by yourself you'd see all the other people who'd ever looked in it as well as you. And I said, not to be left out,

> "When I was going up the stair
> I met a man who wasn't there.
> He wasn't there again today—
> I wish to God he'd go away,"

and by the time I'd finished we had reached the Pembertons' flat. Sir Charles let us in and we all sat down to a scrumptious supper; Lottie seized the opportunity to gorge herself on chocolate cake. As a matter of fact we all did. Then they played card games with

PATRICIA MILES

us and we all watched a comedy film on TV.

Well, you can see we had plenty of things to take our minds off what was going on at home. We stayed till eleven o'clock that night, then Dad came and said Mother and infant were doing well, and thanked the Pembertons, and bundled us into the car.

"Dad, we ought to call the baby Earl Bloggs," said Zach, who was half asleep.

"Who?"

We explained about William Blodgett.

"I don't think we will, somehow," said Dad. "It's a girl."

Mum stayed in bed for about two weeks and Mrs. Korngold really looked after us all. Lots of people's wives from the Institute kept dropping in to see our new baby. Then life gradually went back to normal, but still no sign of Mrs. Korngold leaving.

My general attitude to babies is stand well back from the blue touchpaper; what I mean is, you never quite know what they are going to do next. But I make an exception for close relations. All the same, it was Zach who was most struck with the new baby. I mean, we all liked it—her—but he was really thrilled to the marrow. He kept sticking his finger in her fist and telling her things. Lottie's more like me: I think she still really preferred kittens, and of course ponies—which brings me to Timothy.

Of us three Lottie is always the first to make new friends if we're on holiday or anything, and it was the same here. This time she had palled up with a little girl in her class called Theresa. At every mealtime for days we heard all about Theresa. Theresa's two names—Smith and Jones, with a hyphen in between, viz. Smith-Jones. Theresa's house—a great big house. Theresa's kitten—a really teeny kitten. Theresa's pony.

"... Honestly she has—she's got a pony of her own!"

Theresa's other pony. Theresa's pony that was for sale!!!

The upshot of all this was a conversation between our parents one evening which we weren't supposed to hear, but we did, with Lottie dancing about frantically in the hall saying "Oh, I can't bear it," and "Listen, listen! What are they saying now?" and generally fizzing round the place like an indoor firework.

"If you'd keep still we could hear a lot better," said Zach.

"Hush—the pair of you!" I said.

Then we could hear Dad saying "Isn't it going to be awfully expensive to keep it and feed it and so on?"

"Mrs. Korngold says, if it's used to living out we could keep it in the orchard," said Mum, "and just give it extra hay and pony nuts when the weather turns cold."

"It's cold now if you ask me. Does she know a lot about horses?"

"Seems to. And as she says, we've got a stable if the winter's really bad. Of course, it depends what they're asking for it in the first place. Look," said Mum, "you know very well Lottie never gets her nose out of pony books—she's probably upstairs now reading 'Jane gets a new pony', volume 93—" at this point Lottie went a deep crimson and put her hands over her ears, so she missed it when Mum said "It's not her fault, poor kid. What else can she do? But she's always wanted a pony and I think it's time she had a whiff of reality."

"What does that mean?" asked Zach.

I said, "I think maybe they're going to buy Lottie a pony."

Lottie started listening again. "Oh shut up, you two. I can't hear. What are they saying now?"

Dad was speaking: "Well, I suppose you could take a look at it. It'll need to be a nice quiet pony, though. I don't want Lottie breaking her neck."

"Theresa's been riding it," said Mum. "She's only Lottie's size. I've a feeling they're going to let it go cheap."

"Why? Is there something wrong with it?"

"I don't know; they seem anxious to sell. Oh, there's probably some perfectly harmless reason. And you never know, David, the boys might take up riding too if we had a pony."

(No fear, I thought.)

"Well," said Dad, "you'd better find out how much Mrs. Smith Hyphen Jones wants for it, and if it's not too much we'll have it."

Meanwhile out in the hall Lottie was mouthing "Hooray, hooray, hooray! I'm getting a pony, I'm getting a pony!" I thought she was going off her head. She went into a sort of mindless daze, and went prancing outside in the cold, without her coat, and leaving the door open. Zach ran to shut it—it had begun to get very cold—and I went on listening.

"O.K. then," Mum was saying. "I'll take a look at it anyway, if that's what you think. I'll give them a ring."

When Mum says she'll do a thing she usually means now, so Zach and I scrambled up the stairs p.d.q. True to form, Mum was out in the hall a few minutes later, ringing up and fixing up the inspection for the following weekend.

Saturday came. Dad went back to the lab after lunch—he often does that—and Lottie, Zach, Mum and I walked over to Theresa's house, which stood some way outside the grounds of the stately home.

"It's so nice having Mrs. Korngold," said Mum. "I just trust her completely. I wouldn't have liked to bring the baby out in this."

It was cold. Really horribly cold—and that was about the only thing that day that wasn't Mrs. Smith-Jones's fault. I blame her for all the rest, but I don't suppose I can actually blame her for the weather.

They didn't ask us in to their house, but came down their drive and met us in the road.

"Mum," whispered Lottie urgently when she saw them coming. "Her name's Mrs. Smith-Jones, not Smith Hyphen Jones like Daddy said."

Mum laughed. "So you were listening at the door, little jug-ears. I thought you might be." Then the two mothers introduced themselves, and we set off down the lane.

I don't know if it was to soften us up for the sale or not, but the proceedings began with a spot of the well-known British sport of one-upsmanship, on the part of Mrs. Smith-Jones. "Part" is right—she looked like something out of one of those old black-and-white movies where they have fox-hunting in the middle of summer—all faultlessly got up in posh riding gear. She had smooth fawn hair and she was small and exquisite. Our Mum wore a gray duffle coat. Mrs. Smith-Jones had a tweed jacket and pale fawn breeches to match her hair. Mum had a head-scarf: Mrs. Smith-Jones had a brown velvet riding hat. Mrs. Smith-Jones had brown polished boots to match her hat: Mum was wearing wellies. The same went for the girls—Theresa in riding pants and Lottie in old blue jeans.

"We brought one of Theresa's riding hats for Lottie—we didn't think you'd have one." Mrs. Smith-Jones had a gratingly posh voice. "You're an American, I believe? Do you find you like it here?" She didn't wait for an answer. "Pity you haven't got proper jodhpurs on, Lottie. Never mind. You haven't kept a pony before, have you, Mrs. er Bramble?"

There's no reason why that should sound insulting—I mean most people don't keep ponies—but she made it sound insulting.

Mum said politely: "Why are you selling him?"

Mrs. Smith-Jones immediately seized another chance to show off. "Theresa will be going to boarding school soon—we find that's better—and one pony will be enough for you, darling, won't it?"

"Yes, Mother," said Theresa. "Besides, he keeps getting out and running away." Her mother gave her a dirty look.

By this time we had turned down a narrow lane and then into a car track, which got dirtier and dirtier, till we came to a shed and a five-barred gate in the corner of a small field. The field sloped gently down away from us, and a thick hedge surrounded it. The Smith-Joneses went ahead, and Lottie followed after, eager and tense at the same time, and wearing Theresa's hat.

"That's right," said Mrs. Smith-Jones. "It seems to fit you. Good thing we brought it. You don't want to crack your skull open. Ho ho."

We trooped in behind. Mrs. Smith-Jones went back and checked the gate, as if we hadn't enough sense to fasten it properly. Then she told Theresa to fetch some pony food out of the shed.

A hairy-looking brown thing was standing in the middle of the field by a very small jump. That was Timothy. A milk-white steed he was not.

"He's an easy catch," said Mrs. Smith-Jones. She rattled the bucket Theresa had brought and Timothy pricked up his ears and a split second later he was charging up the field looking something like a cross between an express train and a woolly rhinoceros.

"He's rather greedy," said Mrs. Smith-Jones with a false sort of laugh.

Timothy stuck his head very eagerly in the bucket, and Mrs. Smith-Jones had a quick wrestle with him while she put his head-collar on.

We had a good look at him now he was near to. He had all the equine grace of a kitchen table, and roughly the same proportions, i.e. he was about four feet high and three feet wide. Breed, I should imagine, unknown, though it looked as though a rather coarse doormat might have come into it somewhere. His mane fell in a sort of thicket over his forehead: behind it his eyes glinted out wickedly every now and again.

Theresa took his bucket away, now empty, and tottered back with a saddle which Mrs. Smith-Jones put on him. For the moment he stood quite still and docile, acting meek and cropping the grass. What a dear little pony. Lottie climbed aboard.

"Take him round the field once and then jump him," said Mrs. Smith-Jones.

Mum said, "I think that might be a bit beyond her—she's only had one or two lessons."

"Oh, she'll be all right, it's the pony who does the work. Take him round the field and show him who's boss. Then you can just jump him once."

"But Mummy, you know he ..." said Theresa.

"Hush!"

Lottie set off, very slowly, along by the hedge. In fact, she couldn't get him to move at all until Theresa took hold of his bridle and dragged him away from where he wanted to be—which seemed to be somewhere in the neighborhood of his bucket.

"Clout him!" instructed her mother. Theresa got behind him and clouted. About halfway down the field Lottie managed to get him plodding along on her own. She reached the corner and pulled his head to the left to make him go along the bottom, when a sort of transformation scene took place. It was like looking at a pony Jekyll and Hyde. He came bombing along at the speed of light straight back to us, and the bucket.

I said "I don't think she knows where the brakes are"—rather witty, I thought. Response from Mum: nil. I wondered then if she was scared for Lottie. She didn't say anything. She just quietly put out a hand and gripped my arm. Lottie sort of bucketed to a halt, panting, but quite pleased with herself. Timothy started peacefully cropping the grass again.

When she got her breath back, she said "Now I'm going to jump him."

"Crumbs," said Zach. "It's a good job it's not a long way to fall."

They went off very slowly once more down the field, and this time she actually managed to turn him towards the jump—just as he went into his demon pony act. He took the jump of his own free will, and Lottie fell off his rear end.

"Oh dear, out through the back door," said Mrs. Smith-Jones in a jolly voice. "He's a natural jumper, you know."

My mother caught the reins as Timothy belted past. Mrs. Smith-Jones was quite surprised she had the presence of mind to do that, which gave Mum the chance to say: "Oh, we Americans do a little riding ourselves in the West, you know—we just don't fuss about it so much."

Lottie came stomping up the field. Mrs. Smith-Jones turned on her crossly. "You shouldn't let go of the reins, whatever happens."

Lottie snatched them up. Theresa held Timothy's head for her, and she remounted. For the next twenty minutes—I suppose it only lasted about that long really—Lottie continued to give her impression of a Shrove Tuesday pancake, one that missed the pan every time, i.e. up, over and clunk, splosh, or words to that effect. Each time she scraped herself up off the grass—not leaving go of the reins—and climbed on again. Each time Timothy showed us another clever way of unseating the rider—e.g. (1) gallop very fast, stop dead before jump and rider shoots over nose; (2) jump sideways, remembering to keep all four feet off ground: ride cartwheels in opposite direction—this can be spectacular; (3) stand on forelegs or buck—old-fashioned, this, but tried, trusted and true; (4) stand on hindlegs—never fails; (5) gallop along, turn corner suddenly when rider least expects it; etc. etc. I thought Lottie would have burst out crying by now—she looked pretty near to it once or twice—only she didn't. She's a funny kid. She only cries over the death of King Arthur and Robin Hood and things like that.

All the while Mrs. Jones Hyphen Smith was striding about in her marvelous brown boots, blaring incomprehensible commands in a very loud voice: "Get him on the bit! He's not got enough impulsion! Damn—he's not flexing!" Stuff like that. I don't know if Timothy understood: I'm sure Lottie didn't.

About half way through this performance Mum sort of moaned, but said nothing. I gave her a sweet, which she ate with the paper on. I was surprised to find my stomach churning a bit.

"She might do it all right this time," said Zach. "I think she's getting better. Here she comes." We watched. I can't tell you how horrible it was standing there watching in that rotten field full of big wet thistles and horse manure, with Lottie hammering up towards the jump and clinging on for dear life. This time he did jump it without any tricks. He jumped it clean. It was all right! But only for a moment. He kept on galloping—straight at the hedge.

"She'll be killed!"—that was Mum.

They jumped the hedge—well, not really over it, more sort of through it.

"My God, he's bolted," said Mrs. Smith-Jones, sounding for the first time slightly shaken, but a minute later she was saying to Theresa something about "that's where he gets out, then!" We saw Lottie flash past the gate back down the cart track the way we had come. Then something toppled slowly out of the hedge on to the ground.

"Dear Lord," said Mum, "her hat's come off."

It all seemed to happen very quickly after that. We ran out of the field in time to see Timothy swerve round a distant bend into the lane, his hooves going like pistons. As he swerved, Lottie flew off, head first, on to the cart track. She lay as still as still.

I pelted towards her as fast as I could—Mum couldn't run very well yet after having the baby—but someone else got there before me. Someone coming from the opposite direction. It was Mrs. Korngold. She had come down the lane from the Smith-Jones's house. Timothy, much subdued, was tailing along behind.

When I reached them Lottie's face looked like paper and her body was limp—like a rag doll. Mrs. Korngold had gathered her up in her arms, and Zach and I just stood watching—he'd come up beside me. I didn't think Lottie was breathing.

"Is she …?" I couldn't finish the question.

Mrs. Korngold looked straight at us, only not seeing us at all, and said something. At least she moved her lips, but no sound came out. I was just going to ask Zach what she'd said—he's good at lipreading—when Lottie moved, not all of her, just her eyeballs. You could see them rolling from side to side under the lids, like marbles. Then she jerked her head and took a shuddery breath.

Mum and the Smith-Joneses arrived. Mrs. Smith-Jones had been helping Mum along the road. Mum looked terrible. "Is she all right?"

"Yes, she's all right," said Mrs. Korngold, in a reassuring voice. "See, she's opening her eyes—and don't worry about the baby. Dr. Bramble came home early: he's minding her. Now, my pet …"

Very gently she handed her over to Mum, who had sat down on a fallen log at the side of the track. She took Lottie on her knee and put her good old duffle coat round her, and tried to keep her warm.

"I'll get the car," offered Mrs. Smith-Jones.

"No need," said Mrs. Korngold. "She's coming out of it. Now, what's this all about?" She walked over to Timothy, who stood there strangely obedient. "Well, little one," she said. "I think someone's been giving you oats." She turned to us. "That's like giving alcohol to a pony." She stroked his nose. "You're not bad, are you? You're a little bit tipsy, that's all." She looked sternly at Mrs. Smith-Jones. "What have you been feeding him? You've got him properly oated up." Oh boy, Mrs. Korngold, well done. "Oated up," eh? Keep up the good work.

Mrs. Smith-Jones's jaw dropped. "We have been giving him oats," she admitted.

"I thought so."

Mum said, still hugging Lottie close, "You think he's not a bad pony, then?"

"Oh no," said Mrs. Korngold. "He's a nice pony." She ran an expert hand down his legs and had a look at his teeth: "He just needs proper management."

Oh boy oh boy—I nearly felt sorry for Mrs. Smith-Jones. Mum looked down at Lottie. "Do you still want him, love?"

Lottie nodded her head. "Please can I have him, oh please." She could still hardly speak, but she wanted him all right—passionately.

Some grit. I really admired her. I can just see her in twenty years, sailing single-handed round Cape Horn …

Mrs. Smith-Jones cleared her throat. "We're asking £90, without tack."

Mum looked her in the eye. "I'll give you £45."

Then they haggled a bit, but I don't think Mrs. Smith-Jones's heart was in it, and in the end she said we could have him for £60 plus £25 for tack (that means saddle, bridle etc.: I hope you'll excuse the horsey expressions; I picked a lot of them up later).

Mum said there was no time like the present, put Lottie gently to one side, and got out her checkbook. Mrs. Smith-Jones was so startled she blurted out something about it being wiser to have him properly vetted first, but Mum said she had every confidence in Mrs. Korngold's judgment. I must say, when she's made up her mind my mother doesn't hang about. She wrote the check.

I said I didn't know who was the easy catch, him or us, but Mum only groaned and said, "No jokes Adam, not now, darling, please—I couldn't stand it."

It's funny, she's always saying things like that.

"Come on, Lottie; he's yours now," said Mrs. Korngold. "Don't worry, Mrs. Bramble, he'll be quiet."

Then Lottie scrambled up on him once more, with a bit of help, and actually rode him home—at least she sat on him while Mrs. Korngold led him, and like she said—he was as good as gold.

We turned Timothy out in our orchard, in triumph more or less, but as soon as we got in Mum put Lottie to bed.

I was detailed to bring her up a hot-water bottle. I went off grumbling. "Why me? She looks O.K. now," etc. etc. Actually, of the two of them, I thought Mum looked more shattered than Lottie. I filled the bottle and when I went in with it, sure enough, Lottie was sitting up thoroughly enjoying herself, and scaring Mum half to death by telling her what her last fall felt like. I must say, it sounded interesting.

"At first," she was saying, "it was dark and cold, and a bit misty. There were no walls, nothing you could touch, and I was rushing and rushing—and there was a bird—I think it was an owl—anyway, a big dark bird, beating its wings over my head."

"Don't, darling," said Mum. "I can't bear it."

"Go on," I said.

"Then I sort of slowed down. I came to one of those black iron gates, all with squiggly patterns that you can see through. The sun was shining on the other side and I pushed the gate open quite easily and went in. I found I was in a little grassy place at the edge of a wood, and it was all quite bright and cheerful, and there were wild strawberries growing in the grass. Bright green grass, and bright red strawberries. I was just starting to pick them when I noticed a girl. She had long dark hair and she was watching me out of the trees. She told me to stop picking them and go back home. She wasn't cross or anything, she just looked pale and sad. Then I opened my eyes and saw Mrs. Korngold."

Mum said nothing for a minute, then gave her a kiss and tucked her up and made a fuss over her. "Well, snuggle down now, darling and try to sleep. Mrs. Korngold says she'll teach you to ride. You can have another go on Timothy in the morning, I promise."

Some treat, I thought. But Lottie settled down with an ecstatic smirk on her face. "Oh boy," she said. "It's just too good to be true."

Well anyway—why I'm telling you-in-the-future all this—two things arose from this episode.

1) Mum got it into her head that Mrs. Korngold, grabbing up Lottie when she did, had actually saved her life. After this, as far as Mum was concerned, Mrs. Korngold could do no wrong, and was more firmly dug in with us than ever. And

2) we got another little whiff of her strangeness. I asked Zach what she'd said when she spoke in that queer way, without making a sound. He was a bit vague. "Oh, she just said: 'You shan't have her. Let her go.'"

"Are you sure?"

"I think that was it."

"Let her go?"

"I can't remember. Something like that."

The next one, the next whiff, I mean, was a good bit stronger. As you'll see.

4

AFTER THAT VERY cold day in the field, though it was still only autumn, winter seemed to set in with a vengeance. All the apples in our orchard withered up, and Timothy had icicles hanging off his coat every morning, which in his case meant they practically reached down to the ground. Sometimes the sun came through dully in the afternoons and melted the frost a bit, but by the time I was cycling home from school any bits of me exposed to the air turned slowly blue, and if I took a deep breath the cold air cut into my lungs like scouring powder. Also, the lake was starting to freeze over.

Pretty soon Mrs. Korngold said it was time to bring Timothy in to a stable for the winter. She knew all sorts of strange things about ponies, like feeling the base of their ears to see if they were cold, and only giving them carrots cut lengthwise, so as not to choke them, and I began to feel I wouldn't mind taking a scientific interest in Timothy, but not a soppy girl's one like Lottie.

We didn't pay the weather any particular attention for a while—apart from putting up with it—as we all had our own things to do, and in fact we were all very busy. I'd started making a big map of the grounds of Blodgett Hall. I'd kept the little plan the man on the gate had given us when we arrived, but mine was going to be much better, with little pictures of the hall and the lake and our house. I was coloring it too: the roads, the parkland, everything. You remember that big dark patch we'd seen on the hill behind the stately home? That turned out to be acres and acres of wild garden, with iron railings round it. I'd drawn that in too—we'd found our way into it by now, though we'd hardly begun to explore it properly.

Besides all that, there was school for Zach, Lottie and me, and I suppose even the baby was concentrating on growing or improving her I.Q., or something. You should have seen how virtuous she looked sucking up a bottle of milk.

Dad was busy too: he'd started a new research project with a mathematician to help him—a Dr. Daniels. He didn't get on with him too well but they were both keen on the project, which was to do with shock waves from underground explosions; we could see Dad just starting to get really wrapped up in it.

Mum was working hard preparing her teaching work for the Open University, on *Tom Sawyer* and *Huckleberry Finn*. That's why she hadn't minded moving to another part of the country, by the way, because she can do her work from anywhere. She was hoping to earn enough to pay for having Mrs. Korngold, and not come down on Dad for the money. I expect you've gathered my mother is a brainy type: she used always to be reading *Hamlet* and *Macbeth* to me before I could talk—you may have noticed my amazing vocabulary. She doesn't do it so much to the other two—I got the full brunt of it, as usual.

While she was doing all her deep think stuff Mrs. Korngold ran the house. She'd got the big kitchen range going, and it stayed on night and day. The kitchen was sort of her domain, and she'd made it very homely, with plants in pots and everything very clean and shiny. She'd even got an old white cat, long-haired, that turned up at the back door one day looking bedraggled and lost. Altogether she seemed to have settled in with us more or less permanently, only not like a servant: you could really say she was one of the family now. She still tended to be low-spirited—sometimes she had fits of colossal gloom—but she wasn't sad all the time. She often told Zach stories, and Lottie said she was nearly always out at the gate looking down the road when they got home, no matter how cold it was. At the time Lottie thought she was on the lookout for them—only of course she wasn't. By the time I got home they'd all be nice and cozy in the kitchen, fire blazing, Whitey purring away, and so on.

On this particular evening it was bitter when I was cycling home, but sort of oppressive too. I thought I felt a few drops of icy rain. When I got in, Mum said that if it rained it might get a bit warmer. As if in answer, a flurry of hail struck the window. Still, it was warm enough where we were as we all sat down round the big scrubbed table in the kitchen for our evening meal, Mum, Dad, and everyone except the baby. It was funny: if we ate in the kitchen Mrs. Korngold sat at the head of the table and dished up; if we ate in the dining room Mum did.

"Goody—baked potatoes and cheese," said Lottie. "We had leather-burgers for dinner at school today."

"We had fish," I said, "crêpe soles, actually." I mean, I'm the one who makes the jokes.

Lottie grabbed her knife and fork eagerly and cut her potato in half. "Ugh!" she jerked her chair back in disgust. The inside of the potato was a black squelching mass. Putrescent is the word, I think.

"Hey, look at mine," said Zach. "It's horrible." His was the same as Lottie's. Then Mum, Dad and I each cut into our own potato very gingerly indeed. They were all rotten, squelching rotten, like bad bananas. Everyone was pushing their chairs back from the table.

"There's some white wormy things coming out of the cheese," I added helpfully.

"Yikes!" Lottie let out a screech. "It's all maggoty!" Lottie actually looked as if she were going to cry.

You can imagine, we were all feeling pretty dismal—except for Mrs. Korngold. She had the strangest reaction. She cut her potato in half quite briskly. It was just as bad as ours inside, all black and horrible. For a moment she had a look of cosmic dismay on her face. Then she let out a peal of laughter that would have cracked a chandelier.

Mum pulled herself together. "Bread and corned beef, everyone. Let's hope the bread's all right."

"I have some soup made, too," said Mrs. Korngold, still sort of grinning to herself. "I'll warm it up."

While she was standing over it at the stove Dad said gloomily, "Someone was telling me there isn't a decent vegetable to be had anywhere. It's going to be a hard winter. Fuel's in short supply with this cold weather starting so early: they say there are going to be power cuts."

Mum shook her head at him slightly, meaning, I suppose, "Don't alarm the children."

"Well," she said brightly, "*we'll* be all right with all that frozen food we've got." (We'd brought our freezer north with us, all full of beans and cabbages that we'd grown in Kent.) "And there's plenty of fallen timber in the park. My, that smells good, Mrs. Korngold!"

Mrs. Korngold had started ladling out the soup. She paused with the ladle mid-air. "Listen to the wind getting up."

Even from inside you could hear it lashing the trees, and more heavy drops struck the window.

"Good. That will probably break the cold spell," said Mum firmly.

We ate our supper, which tasted all right this time, did our homework and went to bed. There were a few rumbles of thunder through the evening, but it wasn't till after we'd gone to bed that the storm broke.

A great sheet of lightning and a thump of thunder woke me—the lightning was so bright it came right through your closed eyelids. I pulled a blanket up over my eyes and it even came through that. I wasn't scared of the storm. We weren't on high ground, in fact we were pretty snugly sheltered down by the lake. All the same there was such a racket it was impossible to sleep, and it wasn't long before Zach came creeping in and asked if he could get into bed with me. He had Whitey, the cat, with him, and his feet were like lumps of ice. The storm raged on and on, hail, thunder, and sometimes a dash of half-frozen rain that left icy pellets sliding down the window. After a while Zach fell asleep again, curled round the cat. I felt too cold to sleep and at the same time too frozen to get out of bed and find the eiderdown, which had slid off somewhere. I expect you know how that feels. Every few minutes a great flash lit the room, and I got to thinking it must look pretty spectacular. I went on lying there for a bit, shivering and dozily thinking what a good view of the storm I'd have from the front landing—it looks out over the garden and lake—and in the end I got up and groped my way groggily along.

I wasn't the only one to have the same idea. Mrs. Korngold was standing, fully dressed, by the window. It struck me then that Mrs. Korngold didn't sleep very much, but I wasn't very surprised—as if I'd noticed already, without noticing that I'd noticed, if you see what I mean. I didn't mind sharing the view: I came and stood near her, all friendly, but at the next lightning flash my heart gave a sickening thump. Something was happening to our garden worse than before, when it was writhing about. I felt terribly frightened—all I wanted was to slink back to my room hoping she hadn't seen me. No such luck. Mrs. Korngold caught me by the shoulder and turned me round to face the window. She was sort of gentle but unstoppable, like ice breaking a milk bottle. I daren't look at her, but I suddenly felt that right there beside me she'd suddenly grown *enormous*, like the Statue of Liberty or something.

"Enjoy the storm," she said.

I saw our lake, and the hills and groves beyond it, and beyond them plains and valleys and towns lit up by the lightning. I still daren't glance at Mrs. Korngold. In a way I knew she was her right size, she must have been, because her voice sounded normal and otherwise she'd have gone through the floor or something, but I still *felt* she was huge—both things at once, really. Then the hugeness took over, and I knew I was seeing what she saw, with her vision, so to speak. I stood goggling, with my eyes starting out of their sockets, half-scared to death, but reveling in it in a weird sort of way.

The view widened still further—it was like a huge relief map of the British Isles that you might see in a public library or somewhere, only all real. We saw great jagged mountains, with the lightning striking down into them and the thunder booming against their sides. There was one fearful peak that sprang into three fangs, so clear I thought I'd know it if I ever saw it again. Then the sea, all wild and billowing and throwing itself against a rocky shore.

The storm increased its fury. Whole forests bowed down before it and rose shuddering when it passed over them. Winds howled and shrieked with menace. It was a tempest. It went on and on, but Mrs. Korngold just stood gazing out with a contemptuous calm, defying it. To me it began to feel like sitting in the dentist's chair and wondering if the drill would ever stop (if you have dentist's drills in your time).

I closed my eyes. When I opened them again the lightning was almost continuous and something had changed, but I couldn't tell what. It seemed to me there were fewer towns. Suddenly I saw some strange buildings, sort of futuristic. I can't describe them but I'm sure I was looking into your age.

Then in another prolonged flicker I saw Stonehenge. Good old Stonehenge. But it was broken down, worse than it is now. No it wasn't—it was only half built. There were people working on it, dragging stones on sledges, and in another place woolly mammoths were thundering through the trees. I felt like you do when you step on a step that isn't there—ground gone from under you, I mean.

It was too much.

We'd somehow got loose in time as well as space.

I closed my eyes again and kept them closed. I could feel myself starting to sway. Powerful fingers touched my scalp and held me upright by my hair. I dozed: in my half sleep it seemed gradually as if the storm was easing. When I looked again, it was over.

"Did I fall asleep?"

"Mm? I don't know," said Mrs. Korngold. "Did you?" She looked at me, slightly surprised, I thought, to find me still there. I think she'd forgotten all about me.

I took a timid glance out of the window. The clouds had gone, almost. Moon and stars were shining against a clear dark sky. I could even make out the bold of the silver birch tree by the gate: it gleamed white in the moonlight. The garden had gone back to normal, bushes, everything its ordinary size. Wraith-like wisps of cloud drifted across the moon and a faint nimbus showed all around it, like a washed-out rainbow. I was swaying on my feet with tiredness, then, just when I least expected it, there was yet another terrifying crack of thunder right overhead and at the same time an almighty flash of lightning. Twice more it sounded and with the final flash the tree split. Right down its length from the top to the ground.

I jumped about a foot in the air, and I felt Mrs. Korngold stiffen at my side. Dad said quite loudly in the room next to us "Wha—what's that?" and then apparently went to sleep again, and the baby whimpered a little, then stopped. No one else stirred, and everything grew still once more.

"Listen," I said. I was still shaking with fright. "Isn't that a knock at the door?" The front door was only just below us. Someone had knocked softly with a stick or something, instead of using the bell.

"Go to bed," said Mrs. Korngold. "That will be for me."

A voice called out—a woman's, very clear and pleasant. "Are you listening? I have a message for you."

"What a funny time for anyone to come."

"Yes, isn't it? Go to bed."

I tottered back along the landing. Mrs. Korngold went downstairs and opened the door. I couldn't hear what the woman said but I caught Mrs. Korngold's reply.

"No," she said in a firm voice. "Not till I've seen her again. That's all I have to say. Go back and tell him: my answer is no." The door closed.

For the rest of the night I slept like a log. On both ears, as the French say.

The next day, strangely enough, I didn't want to talk about it to anyone—even Mum and Dad. I can't explain it. I just didn't. I felt sort of jealous of anyone else knowing. I don't know why. Anyway, I persuaded myself, more or less, that I'd dreamt most of it, which wasn't too difficult; after all, it did happen in the middle of the night. And I shut up about it. But I didn't include the birch tree in the dream part. I couldn't: it was there in the morning for everyone to see, split right down the middle.

And another thing; when I combed my hair, my head wasn't half sore—for days

5

"I SEEM TO have lost touch with modern life," said Mum one Saturday about a week after the storm. "Do you know what I feel like having? An orgy of twentieth-century living. I'm going to drive into the nearest big town and cash my trading stamps. Get me the map, Adam."

"Are you sure you feel fit enough?" said Dad. He looked at her doubtfully. She hadn't been all that well lately.

"I feel great—absolutely back to normal," she said firmly, "and what's more, I'm going to throw a party."

We all groaned: now we knew she was her old self again. Mum is more sociable than we are—than Dad, especially. Fourth of July, Thanksgiving, birthdays, any excuse in fact, and Mum has people in.

"What on earth do you want to give a party for, in weather like this? No one in their right mind would want to come out," said Dad, with reason. The weather hadn't improved much after the rain, in fact it was colder, if anything, with thick frosts again every night.

"For a house-warming," said Mum promptly. "House-*warming*"? And she thinks my jokes are bad! "Also, to celebrate our daughter's arrival—and that reminds me. You lot can stop calling her 'baby.' Her name's Beth."

"I like that," protested Zach. "*I* call her Beth."

Lottie said thoughtfully "A for Adam, C for Charlotte" (that's her own proper name). "You've got a long way to go till you get to Z for Zach."

Mum said: "We do not aim to have twenty-six children. We are not working our way through the alphabet. Adam and Charlotte after Dad's parents, and Zach and Beth after mine."

"But you said we were A through Zee."

"That was just a joke, honey."

Dad said: "Listen, don't get off the subject." He made one more effort. "I'm telling you—people won't want to come out in the depth of winter."

"Pooh, call this the depth of winter? A quarter inch of rime on the grass? In any case, they won't have to come far—we'll just have a few people from the Institute."

"All right, all right. Have it your way."

"Thanks, honey, I intend to. Now, Adam, let's see where our nearest Green Shield Stamp depot is: it should tell us on the back of the stamp book."

"I can't really spare the time to go driving around this morning," said Dad. "I've got to go over some stuff that idiot Daniels is taking to a conference. Besides, there's something of my own I want to think about. But I don't feel happy about you going on your own."

"All right, I won't. Can you do your work here?"

"Yes."

"O.K.—You stay in the house and mind the baby, I mean Beth: Lottie and Zach can give you moral support, and I'll take Mrs. Korngold to help me carry things. She might like a trip out; and Adam can do the map-reading."

"Well—if you're sure—that would suit me best," said Dad. So that's how it was settled. The three of us got in the car and the others waved us off, shouting things like "Watch out for ice on the roads," and last minute reminders like "Don't forget to buy candles. We might need them."

"I hope your father will remember to mind Beth properly," said Mum, as we left the grounds and set off for civilization.

Mrs. Korngold chuckled. "Don't worry: she'll remind him."

I can't remember if I told you about Dad being absent-minded? He isn't like that all the time—only when he's got some math problem on the brain, then he's really switched off, like a professor in a comic. He throws his paycheck in the wastepaper basket and puts the empty envelope in his pocket. Things like that. (Actually, the dustbin men found the check and gave it back.) Once, in Kent, he went out to fetch some coal in, and walked four miles along the road carrying an empty coal-scuttle: and another time, when he went out to wash his hands before lunch, he cleaned his teeth, had a bath and put on his pajamas. I read about a man who put his breakfast sausage with his letters on the mantelpiece and blew his nose on his razor. He hasn't done that—yet. Where was I? Oh yes:

Mrs. Korngold said: "Don't worry, Mrs. Bramble, Zach and Lottie are very reliable. You too, Adam, that goes without saying." I must say that gave me a nice warm feeling: also, a queer sense of relief—that she really liked us, I mean.

I was quite glad to get out of the grounds of Blodgett Hall. It gets to be such a little enclosed world on its own, a place like that, with all the same kind of people living there, all brainy scientist types. I sometimes felt the same way when I cycled out of it to school. Also, the trip got Dad and me out of sawing wood, which was good.

Mum had looked quite stricken when she saw our birch tree cloven in half: "What a shame—isn't it a pity—it was a beautiful tree, etc." She went on like that for a bit, then American get-up-and-go took over: "I suppose we'd better cut it down and saw it up for logs." By "we," she meant Dad and me. Mrs. Korngold backed her up and said that was a good idea, as *she* was pretty sure we were going to need it. She was very definite, as if she knew just what she was talking about. So Dad and I had been working at it off and on all week. It was really nice to leave it behind for a bit.

We made good time to the town—due to my superior map-reading—and then drove around for hours looking for somewhere to leave the car. It was a big dirty industrial town with a terrifically solid town hall, built something on the lines of the British Museum. Stone gentlemen in Victorian frock coats stood around outside on pedestals, all a bit grimy. I expect William Blodgett was there glaring at the weather, only we didn't have time to look. The town was full of traffic and harassed-looking people. They all looked pinched and cold, hurrying along to the shops, no one taking much notice of anyone else.

The best we could find in the way of parking was a street of rundown old houses where they'd let you stay "for one hour in any two." There were trees all down the streets with tiny neglected front gardens. It must have been nice once.

Because of the time limit, we had to rush through our shopping, not too easy in a strange town. We didn't dare go back to the car to dump it, for fear of running out of time, so we lugged it all round to the Green Shield Stamp shop with us. Mum grabbed a catalogue and Mrs. Korngold and I minded the shopping bags and looked in the glass showcases at all the marvelous things we could have free.

"Heck!" said Mum in about two minutes. "What do you know! The thing I want" (it was a china tea-set) "has gone up by half a book. That's the only thing I came for."

"Maybe we have enough extra with what we've bought today?" said Mrs. Korngold. She pulled a handful of stamps out of one of our bags and started licking and sticking as fast as she could, but we were still a few pages short.

"I know!"—this was me—"I saw one of those big supermarkets with a treble Green Shield Stamp offer all this week."

"Where?"

"Quite near here. You could fill up the book."

Mum took a deep breath. "We'll do it," she said. "I'm not coming all this way for nothing."

It wasn't a bit like our usual shopping, where we just get what we need as we go along, as we don't exactly live rich. Mum kept saying things like "Do you think I could do with half-a-dozen best linen glasscloths? Yes, I could," and so on. She paid up with a credit card, and we hurried back in triumph to the stamp shop, where we joined a queue. It was a very slow queue. I was gazing round for the umpteenth time when I noticed the clock.

"Mum! Had you forgotten the car?"

"Oh my God! We must be well over the limit." Mum sort of sagged all over: she looked suddenly very tired. "What's the fine nowadays? Six pounds? Oh boy," she said bitterly, "some free gift this turned out to be!" She really looked defeated. "Well, I guess we might as well stay here now."

I knew how she felt—like when you kill yourself running for a bus, and it pulls away from you just as you get there. For a minute I thought she was going to cry.

She made an effort. "If you stay here, I'll move the car … Oh, what's the use? I shan't find anywhere to park, and we'll probably never find each other again …"

"Wait." Mrs. Korngold rallied round. "What about this for an idea? You stay and we'll go back to the car. They might not have spotted us yet, and they probably won't fine us if there's somebody sitting in the car. Come on, Adam."

She seized the heaviest bag—I picked up the other two—and

we raced back through the crowded streets with Mrs. Korngold keeping up very well for her bulk and age, whatever that was, and swerving nimbly round the Saturday afternoon shoppers. I put on a spurt and belted ahead, round the corner and into the street with the trees where we'd left the car.

"It's all right!" I waited for her to catch up. "I don't think there's anything stuck to the windscreen yet." (They usually put the summons under the wipers.) "Oh, rats!" I could suddenly see a man in a navy blue uniform making his way slowly along behind a woman with a pram, a family with young children, all spread out across the pavement, and a smart soldierly-looking old age pensioner. "Here comes a blooming traffic warden! I'll tell hi Mum's just coming." I raced off again.

"Adam!"

I glanced back for a moment at Mrs. Korngold. I remember suddenly thinking how handsome she looked. Her fresh-colored skin had a bloom like a peach and her blue eyes flashed with anger. She put out her free hand in a curious gesture and snapped her fingers, and when I looked up the street again there was just this dog barking at our car, and *no traffic warden in sight at all.*

I stood gaping for a moment at the space, so to speak, where the warden had been … where the dog was now. I mean—it would be very nice if you had someone on your side who could just get you out of trouble by … well, I could see for myself that what I at first thought was plain impossible. I mean, you couldn't see clearly all the way up this street, what with the trees and the people … I must just have been mistaken, that was all. There can't have been any traffic warden.

Thankfully, we put the stuff in the car. The dog watched us. Mrs. Korngold smiled and patted him. He was a nice little fellow, a black-and-white rough-haired terrier with one white ear and one light brown.

"Good dog," she said, and he wagged his tail.

Gosh, was Mum relieved when she got back, free gift and all!

"Let's get the hell out of this burg," she said, all cheerful again. I looked back as we drove off: the dog was still there on the pavement, wagging its tail.

Once our Dad was driving along a country lane, and he stopped and ran back because he thought he'd seen a dead pheasant on the road, and he knew Lottie would like the feathers. But when he got there it was just a dirty bundle of rags. An optical illusion. I suppose anyone can deceive themselves. Honestly, it was the only explanation I could think of at the time for that traffic warden: I reckoned I'd invented him.

A few days later Mum threw her party. Some party!

It started in the usual way about half-past eight, with Zach, Lottie and me all being put on our best behavior to take people's coats, hand round nuts, etc. which we did—all very normal and friendly. Then Lottie and Zach went to bed, and I hung around upstairs for a bit listening to Lottie read Zach a story. In a little while I drifted down again, hoping to raid some of the interesting eats while the adults were knocking back the booze. The house seemed to me to have got very crowded, and Mrs. Korngold still kept going to the door and letting in more and more strange people. Perhaps there weren't so many really, it may have been just that they were rather large people. There was a very distinguished-looking person in naval uniform I'd never seen in my life before, and a tall imposing lady with very gray eyes who said she was his sister. I heard Mum say to Dad "Who *are* all these people? They're not students, are they? They look rather mature for students."

"I don't know who they are … They're not from my department, that's for sure."

Mum laughed, a kind of merry I-have-been-at-the-punch-bowl

laugh, and said, "You're so absent-minded I bet you've been working with them for the last month and haven't noticed. Anyway, it doesn't matter, they're all perfectly charming people, and what's more, they've all very kindly brought presents." So they had, stuff to drink—which they just poured into the punch-bowl—and little baskets of cakes.

"My dear Mrs. Bramble," said Sir Charles, who was chief guest. "What hospitality! Nectar and ambrosia!"

"How very curious you should say that," said the lady with the gray eyes.

I crept back upstairs with a cake for each of us. Zach had gone asleep, with Whitey curled up beside him, so Lottie and I shared his.

"Where did Mum get these cakes?" said Lottie.

"I don't know: I think some of the guests brought them."

"Gosh, they're scrumptious!"

We sneaked down for more. They were the sort of thing that once you'd tasted you couldn't leave alone. Do you know what I mean? Some people call it "more-ish." These cakes were the most more-ish things we'd ever tasted.

We sat on the stairs nibbling, in an unobtrusive sort of way (we hoped), and that was how we came to hear a queer snatch of conversation which came floating out of the kitchen.

"No, thank you," Mrs. Korngold was saying, in a firm voice. "I like the Bramble family and they've been very kind to me. I shall stay here with them."

Another voice, male, said: "Won't you *please* come back with us?" Then a female voice, soft and pleading: "Oh please—won't you? What about your work?"

There was a pause, then Mrs. Korngold replied: that nothing they had to say mattered to her in the slightest, that she had lost all interest in her work, and that she wasn't going anywhere with them until they knew what.

Lottie said "What are they supposed to know? What's going on? Who's that talking to her? Are they inviting Mrs. Korngold to go somewhere?"

"They've got a nerve," I said. "It's them—some strange people from the Institute who've turned up. I think they're trying to pinch her off us."

"I bet she won't go," said Lottie.

The voices rose in the kitchen.

"You know what I want," cried Mrs. Korngold. "Nothing short of that will persuade me. I don't care who sent you!" Her voice sort of cracked, with a sob in it.

Lottie clutched my arm. "Listen! They're making her cry!"

"Shall we go in and show we're on her side?" I muttered, not moving. For some reason my legs had turned to lead.

"Yes," said Lottie, not moving either.

"Oh, come on." I got up and dragged her along with me.

I just had my hand on the knob of the kitchen door—Lottie was clinging on to me—and I don't know why, but my heart was pounding and you know that nerve I've got in the back of my knee—it was jumping; when all at once there was a mighty peal of thunder right over the house. I nearly jumped out of my skin. I can tell you, it was so loud it rattled our teeth: I felt the door shake (and Lottie), and the knob sort of jarred in my hand. Talk about living in the thunderstorm belt of the British Isles—Dad hadn't mentioned that either, when we moved. Crikey—as if that wasn't enough—all the lights went out.

Behind us the sitting-room door burst open. Everyone was walking and laughing, and flicking on cigarette lighters, and wondering was it an electricity failure caused by the lightning, or was it a power cut at last, as we'd been promised by the Ministry of Fuel.

Mrs. Korngold came briskly out of the kitchen with a lit candle and passed us by. Behind her, in the glow of the kitchen fire, loomed two dark shapes. They seemed huge. For a minute they remained quite still.

Some powerful instinct kept Lottie and me equally still—just hoping not to be seen, I think. I know nothing in the world would have made me go into the kitchen just then. I actually felt the hair on the nape of my neck sort of bristle. Then one of the figures stirred a little and said "Well, if she won't she won't. There's nothing more we can do at the moment."

"Very well," agreed the other. "We'll leave it for now. We'll just have to try something else later."

A coal fell in the grate and a shower of sparks went up. I drew a breath—I hadn't noticed I'd stopped breathing. Beside me I could feel the tension going out of Lottie. We crept back down the hall.

A moment or two later Dad started investigating the fuse-box by the front door with an electric torch. We began rushing about very helpfully, putting candles in candlesticks and finding matches. Of course, in the end Dad spotted us and said "Bed, you two," and off we went, with Lottie looking like something out of a nursery rhyme, with her long nightie and a candle in her hand.

I lay awake for a long time, listening to the party which seemed to be going on more hilariously than ever down below. After a while I got up and tried the switch. The power was still off. Soft flakes of snow began to hit my window.

6

THE SNOW THAT began on the night of the party continued off and on for the next few days. It wasn't very deep but there were the usual traffic hold-ups and panics and then they started gritting the roads and everyone struggled back to their usual routine as best they could. We had some good snowball fights at school and made a super slide in the school yard which all the masters were careful to avoid (drat, curses, etc.)—but actually it wasn't very long now till the end of term.

We were all having breakfast one morning (boiling hot porridge followed by kippers) when Mum put down a letter she'd been reading and said:

"I'm glad it's snowed. It'll be just right for having Crispin."

"Crispin—is he coming? Ugh! What a start to the holidays!" One of us said it, it doesn't matter who because we all felt the same, including Dad.

"Look how it works out," Mum breezed on. "If the weather gets too bad, you'll have a friend right here in the house to play with, and if it's fine you'll have something to go out and do, build snowmen or something."

Lottie asked gloomily "How long is he staying for?"

"Two weeks."

"Two weeks!" Universal groans.

Dad said it was little short of foolhardy to leave the lad with people who actually had a deep lake to hand.

This Crispin is the son (I nearly wrote "sun," and that might be nearer his mother's view of him) of my father's sister, i.e., our Aunt Cecilia. She's the one who's supposed to be very beautiful—she has soppy brown eyes: she is also a child psychiatrist. In age Crispin comes between Lottie and Zach. Dad says the really annoying thing about him is that due to his corny upbringing he'll probably turn out to be the most marvelous sane well-balanced adult that ever lived, while we'll be a load of delinquents. In the mean time, a more unmitigated little tick it would be hard to find. More of this later. I will refrain from comment on his name, as it is not his fault—except to say that it suits him. My mother says Aunt Cecilia probably chose it to bolster his sense of his own individuality, as he won't meet many other people with a name like that, and that's true enough.

It turned out Aunt Cecilia was going to a conference of child psychologists in Switzerland. (I'm sorry I have to keep calling her Aunt Cecilia—it's a bit of a mouthful, isn't it? But she won't have "Celia"; or even "Cecily": she insists on her full name; she has a thing about it. All I can say is it's a good thing none of us lisps.) Anyway, she thought that while she was gone it would be better for Crispin to live in a house with other children, i.e. us (moan groan), rather than stay at home with his Dad, who is an engineer (and all right), and Mum agreed. Or as she tactfully put it to us: "You can cut out the drama, you guys—he's coming."

Honestly, my Mum never learns—she will invite people to stay, completely forgetting how much she hates it. Parties, yes; looking after visitors—no. She can just about put up with us because we belong to her, and besides, we are extremely independent. Crispin, on the other hand, takes a lot of looking after. For example, he was staying with us once when he was younger, and every time he got dressed or had been to the loo or something, he had to have each layer of his clothes, vest, pants, etc., all perfectly smoothed down in the right order under each other. It took our Mum ages, and he wouldn't let her stop till she got it quite right. I have to admit, he does always look tidy, unnaturally tidy, not like Zach and me who usually go round with our shirt tails hanging out.

Maybe Mum thought it would all be different now we'd got Mrs. Korngold. It was different all right.

Well, he arrived, in a snazzy little sports car driven by his mama. Aunt Cecilia didn't even take her fur coat off, as she was rushing for her plane. She just came in and chatted to Mum for a bit, and admired Beth, while Crispin took his things upstairs and changed into his slippers. It seemed to me he was taking his time, if his mother was in a hurry. At last the door opened and there he stood, all neat and clean. A powerful blast of mother-love, sickening to behold, went beaming across the room at him from Aunt Cecilia's soppy brown eyes. Honestly, I was surprised it didn't knock him down: he's only a weedy little squirt. (I can tell you, I'm jolly glad our mother doesn't look at us like that for everyone to see.) Anyway, pretty soon after that we were waving goodbye to Aunt Cecilia.

Now, in case you're beginning to feel sorry for Crispin and think we were all set to be mean to a poor little kid far from home, we weren't. Mum had told us not to. But I will just tell you why he got us down. (By the way, I trust you-in-the-future aren't somebody like him! No, of course not. There couldn't be anyone else quite so incredibly irritating.) His most annoying trick was, he always had to be right. Also, he was greedy. He was the sort of kid you expected to see standing on a stool at the pantry door reaching down a pot labeled "JAM." Next, he had an uncanny flair for hitting on the one thing with each of us that most got under our skin. And last, he was bone idle: he wouldn't do a thing for himself if he could possibly help it, let alone for anyone else.

Oh well, I thought, maybe he's changed. But he hadn't. That afternoon, Mrs. Korngold set us down to a good spread, sardines on toast, boiled eggs, biscuits, cakes, jelly. (Dad was eating with Mum later.) True to form, Crispin ate and ate. We're fairly hearty eaters ourselves, but there are limits.

Zach said admiringly "Do you know, Crispin, you're the only person who's come to our house and eaten as much as us."

Crispin licked his fingers. "Are there any more of those chocolate biscuits?"

Crikey, I thought, it's like having a termite to stay. Mrs. Korngold said "Don't you think you've had enough?"

"You're still eating," he said cheekily—which I must admit she was—"so can I have one?"

"No, you'll make yourself sick."

"No I won't, I'm never sick."

"It's still 'no'."

"Well, can I have another cake then?"

"No. You've had enough."

It seemed to me a distinctly edgy note had crept into Mrs. Korngold's voice. We got down pretty smartly after that. Then we pushed off to the sitting-room and got out the Monopoly, and the minute the lid was off Crispin grabbed the battleship, double quick, in case anyone else wanted it. Actually I like the top hat, Lottie always chooses the dog, and Zach picks the old boot, I don't know why.

Mum watched us for a while: she was sitting by the fire with Beth on her knee. After a bit, Crispin commented "She hasn't got much hair, has she?"

"No, not yet," said Mum.

We played on.

"Are you going to put a gate at the top of the stairs?"

"No," said Mum, "I don't think so." (It's funny how often "no" comes into conversations with Crispin—I didn't notice that till just now, when I was writing it.)

"Your baby might fall down. We had a gate at the top of our stairs."

"I dare say," said my mother, in a strained sort of way, "but we don't believe in that sort of thing, we don't think it's necessary."

"You just let us fall downstairs," said Lottie to me under her breath.

"I heard that Lottie," said Mum.

You see? He makes everyone quarrelsome. I don't know how he does that. Just a gift, I suppose.

The evening wore on, as the saying goes: it was ertainly wearing.

Next day we three went to school—we still had about half a week to go before the winter holidays; they were starting earlier than normal to save fuel. The first night, when she got home Lottie nearly had a fit: she found Crispin feeding Timothy rounds of carrots, though she had specifically told him not to. He just said he thought she was wrong.

The second night Zach actually burst into tears. While he was at school Crispin had found his Boeing 707 that he made out of purple plasticine (it was absolutely horrible, but it had a lot of detail on which took Zach ages, and he was very proud of it). Crispin had squashed it up and remade it into a bunch of violets (which were just about as lovely as the airplane).

On the following evening, when I went upstairs to my room, well …! You know I told you what Lottie liked most about our house was the stables and Zach liked the lake? Well, I like the house itself and especially having my own room, and I'd gone to some trouble to keep other people out of it. I'd put a drawing of a huge eye on the door, and a sign which said "Big Brother is Watching You," and a "Keep Out on Pain of Death" notice, with a skull and crossbones. Did this deter Crispin? Oh no. He'd gone in and touched and muddled everything, my designs for a space-ship (there were pages of that), my plastic moon-probe—everything. My new rocket was lying in bits on the floor.

I keep quite a lot of things lying about, models, map-making stuff and so on—things I've not quite finished making, so they're all spread out. I tend to get a bit side-tracked. I think that shows I've got a lively mind, open to new interests etc., but my mother says it's because I don't concentrate on anything long enough.

"Follow-through," she calls it. It's not enough to have "get-up-and-go," she says, you've got to have "follow-through-till-it's-done" as well. "When you put your hand to the plow … etc. etc." Like our Dad, I suppose. He often works on the same hard sum for months. I don't know how he does it. Anyway, as I say, the thing I minded Crispin mucking about most was my moon-probe and my designs for a space-ship, planned, drawn and invented by me.

To tell you the absolute honest truth, and I wouldn't like anyone else to know this, but I don't mind telling you, I'd like to go into space myself. I'd like to go to Cambridge and then the Massachusetts Institute of Technology, and get into Space Research.

I came down the stairs, three steps at a go, ready to commit murder. Unfortunately, Mum was there and I had to spare my cousin's wretched life. He said he'd just gone in to look for a book, and it was all in a muddle, and most of the things were on the floor anyway. I said that was where I kept them—on the floor—and I understood the muddle, till he'd got in among it. Mum said it was my own fault for not having more control over my possessions, and that Crispin wasn't much to blame, as there wasn't a lot for him to do on his own. Strewth!

Then it was supper time. It was a very memorable meal, I can tell you. "What's that smell?" said Dad as he sat down. "It smells like burnt cabbage." That was the start.

Now Mrs. Korngold had been heard muttering to herself something about "fish and guests both stink after three days," and I think Crispin had triggered off one of her fits of gloom, which after all were always pretty near the surface, only we'd got used to them. They usually made her cooking go off a bit. On this occasion she served: burnt chops, burnt runner beans, burnt potatoes, followed by burnt pancakes. The cabbage never appeared at all, except as an evil miasma.

Mrs. Korngold wasn't eating with us that night. She wouldn't. She'd laid the meal in the dining room and Lottie and I had to run in and out fetching and carrying. The first time we went in we saw her scraping Dad's cabbage into the waste bucket. His wonderful cabbage that he'd grown himself on organically composted soil! It had boiled dry and stuck to the pan. Mrs. Korngold gestured towards the table with a despairing hand, and we took in the dishes. Such a cloud of misery enveloped her we didn't dare say a word, but it wasn't very long before, back in the dining room, Dad was raising the roof.

"Aged twit! She'll have to go. It's no use, she'll have to go!"

Mum was asking him to keep his voice down and doing her best to shut him up. "Mrs. Korngold is a superior person, and I won't have her spoken about like that."

"Well, look at my beans! They took six months to grow—and half an hour to ruin," etc. etc.

The meal dragged to a close, and I think their coffee was all right. Things calmed down a bit. We went away and watched TV, and in a little while Mum brought us up cocoa and biscuits. Then the power went off, and I don't know about Mum and Dad but we all decided we'd had quite enough of that day and took ourselves off to bed.

Next morning, Mum had just torn the wrappings off a boring-looking periodical (no pictures in it) which she gets by post, and always greets with cries of joy—it's something to do with her work—when Crispin came crossly downstairs.

"There's a button missing off my shirt."

"Put something else on," said Mum, hopping off quick into the study. He followed her relentlessly.

"I want to wear this one."

"Mm? What's that? Haven't you got another shirt?"

"Yes, I have."

"Well, go and put it on, love."

She sat down and started to read the front page. She reads in a funny way, every few lines she looks up and gazes into space—deep think, deep think—then "Dive! Dive! Dive!" so to speak back into the close print. I was quietly deciphering a letter from my French pen-friend and wondering why he always wrote to me on graph paper with purple ink, when Crispin managed to interrupt again, very effectively. He'd raised the lid of the piano and was pressing the same two keys—very high up and right next to each other— quite softly but over and over. It was like the ancient Chinese water torture.

Mum surfaces slowly out of her article. "Are you still here? What is it you want, Crispin?"

"I like this shirt best," he said. "I've got the button for you to sew on."

I don't quite know what Mum was going to say next—she opened her mouth, then closed it in time. I hardly liked to see a parent go that purple color. Whoops, Crispin, *mon brave*, you are now entering an area of high voltage … you have passed into the danger zone … but Crispin didn't seem to notice: some people just don't have that kind of radar.

"Bally well put it on with the button missing," I said.

Lottie came wandering in in her vest and pants. "What's missing?" she asked, having caught the tail end of the remark.

"The button off Crispin's shirt."

"It's not missing, I've got it here," he piped up.

"Leave it there, I'll sew it on," said Mum. She'd got a grip on herself and the purple color had faded. Her tone was calm, almost pleasant.

"Well, will you do it now?"

"In a minute."

"But I want to wear it."

! ! !

Lottie and I exchanged an appreciative glance.

"What do you want to wear?" said Zach. He came in with a piece of buttered toast in his hand.

Mum looked round with a hounded look on her face as all her darling children clustered about her. (She still had her finger on the bit she wanted to read.)

"I've told you, don't eat toast in here, Zach! And I've told you before, Lottie, don't wander round half dressed!"

"Is something the matter?" said Zach.

Crispin explained about his button.

"Oh, is that all?" said Zach scornfully. "Come on—I'll sew it on for you. I'm good at sewing buttons …" he led Crispin away.

"Of all the dratted pains in the neck—for pity's sake get that child out of the house for a bit, before he sends me insane," said Mum.

Smug was how we felt. "What did we tell you?" said Lottie.

I said "He's good at getting his own way, isn't he? I expect Aunt Cecilia's been building up his confidence or something."

"She sure has!" said Mum, and then—just as she prepared to submerge—"I'm warning you—don't you ever behave like that in someone else's house!"

Now I ask you—what had we done?

We didn't exactly go out for a while. First we finished breakfast and messed about for a bit in the house in a nice free-and-easy way, because we were on holiday too, now. Then we spent a bit of time watching Mrs. Korngold cutting a chocolate cake in layers and putting filling in—we helped cream the filling, lick bowls, etc. She liked us helping. Afterwards she mixed two colors of icing. She spread the white icing first, then put some pink icing in a little bag with a hole in the corner. She gave Lottie the bag and told her to squeeze it, and write anything she liked on the cake. Lottie thought for a minute and then took the bag and wrote EAT ME, and Mrs. Korngold put it away in the larder for tea. I think she was trying to make up for the previous night's supper. Anyway it looked as if we were going to have a slap-up tea. She was like that, was Mrs. Korngold—all or nothing.

Then Mum came in and told us all to clear out, now, instanter and at once, and we wrapped up warm because of the snow, and went off to the wild wood.

Well, that's what we called it sometimes. It wasn't a wood at all really, it was just Earl Blogg's gardens. You remember? The ones that made the dark patch behind the house. And they weren't meant to be wild, they'd just got that way.

They were really something, these gardens, they covered acres of steep hillside behind the Earl's stately home, and we'd still only explored part of them. We decided to show Crispin the part we knew.

"Let's go to the blue pool," said Lottie.

"Yeah! Come on, Crispin, you'll like it, it's a magic wood," said Zach.

"Why is it magic?"

"Because of the blue pool."

"There's lions in the wood, too," said Lottie.

"No, there aren't," I said.

"Well, there used to be in the olden days." She'd picked this bit of information up at school.

"What? Running about loose?" said Crispin.

"Yes, all over the gardens they used to be—and I know that's true, or why are there railings all round? So there."

What Earl Bloggs had done, Dad said, was to take this slope of Derbyshire moorland and cover it with rare flowering shrubs from the Himalayas, and some English trees, mostly evergreens, and millions of daffodils and narcissi. (Of course we hadn't seen those yet, but we would in the spring.) And Dad told us he'd brought in an army of gardeners from Spain or somewhere, and stonemasons to build paths and grottoes and bridges. Only now all the bushes had sort of escaped and turned themselves into a jungle, and half the paths were grown over, and a lot of stonework was damaged. And no one went there but us, so we pretended it was ours.

(As a matter of fact, you know that big map of the grounds I was drawing? I'd changed my mind about it a bit and decided just to concentrate on the wild garden.)

We had a great time fuddling Crispin with information and showing off all the way up the hill. Then we came to our usual gap in the fence and squeezed through, with me leading.

"Ouch! Watch out for the branches swinging back," I said, a snowy rhododendron having just socked me in the face. Then we pushed our way through thick bushes up to one of the paths that were cut out like giant steps in the side of the hill. We were boiling hot, so we all ate some snow—there were about four inches on everything, rhododendrons, Christmas trees, the lot.

"Gosh! It's like fairyland, isn't it?" said Lottie. "Hey! I wonder if the little waterfall's frozen?" We hurried on.

"Look! It's all icicles."

"I wish the sun would come out and make the icicles glitter," said Zach; and then it did, for a little while. I think at that moment none of us, even Crispin, would have wished to be anywhere else on earth but in that snowy wood in Derbyshire. I mean, we'd lived in Kent, which is called the Garden of England, and all that—but the wild garden had something else. It was—well—wilder.

"I bet this place is better now than when it was new," said Lottie.

"And I bet Earl Bloggs would have liked it better too," said Zach.

"And I bet he wouldn't," I said. "He liked taming things—like those lions."

That reminded Lottie to go on with her theory. "Well, you see, Crispin, those lions married and had some baby lions, and when their mother and father went off to live in a zoo, no one knew about the little lions, and they grew up and had some more lions, and …"

Crispin interrupted her. "What do they live on?"

"Rabbits," said Zach.

"I don't believe any of it," said Crispin. "Why are there no lion footprints?"

He had a point there—it was a good day for the footprints; you could see them quite clearly in the snow: rabbits', birds', even deer's—but no lions'.

"They don't come in this part, clever dick," said Lottie.

"Huh," said Crispin scornfully. "When do we get to this blue pool, then?"

"It's by the waterfall," said Zach.

"But we've seen the waterfall."

"That was just the little one," said Zach proudly. "You just wait. It's like a great big gorge, where we're going."

"Yeah—it's fantastic," said Lottie.

"Yeah—it's great." Lottie and Zach kept this up for a while, and we went on, forcing our way along the path, and beginning to get a

PATRICIA MILES

bit cross as the branches kept whipping back in our faces. The sun went in. Every now and then we passed a grotto, a kind of stone garden house, with crazy paving in front of it. I was thinking they looked just a bit sinister, all overgrown and damp. Then suddenly we came out into the open; we had reached the ravine.

I supposed there had once been just an ordinary moorland stream falling down the hillside. Now it leapt off a man-made precipice, fell into a pool—on the level where we were standing—flowed under a stone causeway and cascaded another twenty feet down to a larger pool with a bridge over it. It was a stunning place: awe-inspiring, really.

There was a sheet of ice on the blue pool. Lottie usually says this is where the lions came down to drink, only she didn't this time, but she broke the ice.

"Is that it?" said Crispin, staring at it critically. "It's not really blue, is it? It's a sort of dirty green."

Zach said "It goes blue when the sun's shining."

A few feeble rays shone above our heads at the top of the gorge, but not enough to turn the green water blue.

"Oh," said Crispin, losing interest and going on across the causeway. "What's down there?"

"Only that other pool and the bridge," I said. "It's quite near the bottom edge of the grounds. We don't bother with it."

"There's some steps by the waterfall," said Crispin. He was right—but they were all broken and uneven. "Let's go down."

I don't like those steps. I don't know if you will ever have read a book called "Kidnapped"—we had to read it at school—but there's a bit in it where the hero has to climb a stone staircase with a great drop on one side. He goes up in the dark, and one of these steps is missing, and he sort of senses he's going to be killed and just stops in time. These steps gave you exactly that sort of feeling, though of course it wasn't dark—yet. Still, what with the snow and ice, they were nasty and slippery and dangerous. I thought of Aunt Cecilia trusting Crispin to us and said "no" very firmly. For once Crispin didn't argue, and we set off back.

I went first, bending down under low branches and trying not to knock the snow in Lottie's face, then came Zach, and then Crispin. When I got to a more open bit by one of the stone houses, I waited.

"Where's Crispin?"

He was no longer following behind. We hung about for a few minutes—still no sign of him.

"Stay here, you two," I said. "I'll get him."

I went back a few yards and yelled "Crispin!" In a minute Lottie and Zach came hurrying after me.

"I've just thought," said Lottie, "I bet he's gone down to the other bridge. He wanted to."

Just what he would do. "Well," I said, "there's no sign of him here. Didn't you notice him drop behind, Zach?"

"No, I didn't."

We went all the way back to the blue pool, calling his name and shouting, but all we got back was the echo.

"He's not here," said Lottie in a scared voice when we arrived at the gorge.

"I can see that," I said. "He isn't on the bridge either." I was trying to keep calm. We stood on the causeway between the pool and the big cascade. We gazed up and down the ravine, but we couldn't see him. The ice had formed again where Lottie had broken it for the lions. "You don't think he's in the pool?" she quavered.

"No, of course not. We'll try the steps."

"Yikes! Watch out," yelled Zach. "It isn't half slippy on these stones."

"I wish I hadn't got my wellies on," wailed Lottie. "I keep skid-ding."

We went across the narrow causeway of stones to where the steps began. "Look—that's his footprint!" said Zach.

"He stood there before," I said.

"There's another one lower down! We'll easy find him now."

"I'll go first," I said. "Don't come rushing behind."

"I don't like it," moaned Lottie, and I didn't blame her. There was a sheer drop over the ravine on one side, and bank shored up with a dry stone wall on the other.

"You can hold on to these tufts of grass sticking out of the wall," I said, "And take your time."

We went down carefully, as far from the edge as possible, but Crispin's brave little footsteps went right down the center of each step—all the way to the bottom—all the way on to the bridge.

Once we got down there I could see at once there was something badly wrong.

"Keep back, you two."

"Why? What is it? Have you found him?"

"Shut up a minute."

There's a poem Dad knows by Wordsworth about a little girl called Lucy who gets lost on the moors in the snow. They trace her footsteps to a bridge over a river.

> *Then downward from the steep hill's edge*
> *They tracked the footmarks small;*
> *And through the broken hawthorn hedge,*
> *And by the long stone wall.*
>
> *They followed from the snowy bank*
> *Those footmarks, one by one,*
> *Into the middle of the plank,*
> *And further there were none!*

All this went whizzing through my head in a useless sort of way, because it was just the same as Crispin's. His footsteps went as far as the middle of the bridge, and "further there were none." Of course, there wasn't much rushing river below, just a wide pool choked with dead soggy leaves, but there were boulders in it you could split your head on. I lay down in the snow with my head sticking over the edge. I don't know what I thought I'd see in the water. Lottie started bawling his name again—then burst into tears, which you know is rare for her, and she set Zach off. You've never seen such cold wretched miserable kids as we were.

Then Crispin stepped out from a big clump of laurels on the steep bank above the wall. "April fools," he yelled.

Of course, it was only the middle of December.

"I faked the footprints," he said. "I walked backwards, I stepped in each footprint twice. Did you think I was dead?"

Lottie and Zach still had their mouths wide open, but no sound came out. It was like watching TV with the volume switched off. I got up off the cold ground, and tried to think of the most cutting thing I could—then he suddenly lost his footing on the tufty grass and came slithering down the hill with a howl of fright. He scrambled up again and said "I was going to roar like a lion but I thought I mightn't get it right. You would have seen where I climbed up the wall if you'd looked."

Lottie got her voice back and said he was a horrible pig, and Zach said he wished he *had* fallen in. I thought of a few choice comments too. We went all the way home like that, us furious and Crispin quite pleased with himself. From time to time he tried out a lion's roar. It was rotten.

We were pretty quiet at lunch and afterwards we scattered to our favorite parts of the house. We'd had enough of being together for a while.

About the middle of the afternoon I started to get a bit peckish. It wasn't teatime for ages, but I went along to the kitchen, and Mrs. Korngold told me to help myself to some biscuits out of the larder. Our larder is like a long thin room you walk into. I went in and started rummaging around.

"Don't touch the cake," she said in a joking voice.

"I won't. Er—what cake?"

"What? What are you saying?"

"There's no cake here. There's an empty plate with crumbs on."

I brought it out and we both stared at it.

"Well, I'll soon settle him." Mrs. Korngold didn't waste any time speculating. She just opened the door into the hall and called out: "Crispin! Come down here."

He answered her at once in his high clear voice. "What is it? What do you want?" He must have been on the stairs: I couldn't see because Mrs. Korngold was blocking the door.

"You ate the cake that was for tea, didn't you?"

"What if I did?" he said cheekily. "You can make another. Anyway, it said EAT ME, so I did."

"Come here," roared Mrs. Korngold, "you impudent little boy! What did you say to me?"

"I said you could make another," he answered, with a very slight quaver in his voice. "There's plenty of time."

"What do you know about cake-making, greedy child—all you know about is cake-eating."

"Well, that's not my job, it's yours," he said, cheeky as ever. I almost had to admire him. Crumbs, though, I thought, he's done this time.

Then, strangely enough, Mrs. Korngold laughed, a nice, mellow, fruity laugh. "You like licking your lips, don't you? Well, lick them some more."

What a funny thing to say, I thought. I heard Crispin start to say something back, but whatever it was I lost it, because a great burnt-out coal toppled down in the fire just then and broke into little bright bits of flame. I suppose I thought Crispin had run off upstairs again—if I gave it a thought—because after that there was, for a moment, total silence.

Then Mrs. Korngold looked back at me over her shoulder and said in her usual calm voice, "Don't let the fire die down, Adam. I'm going upstairs for a while."

She closed the door. I put a bit of coal on and sat down at the table with a few biscuits and a book. Bliss. Peace and quiet at last.

About five minutes later Zach wandered into the kitchen. "Hey, look, Adam."

"Go away."

"No, look."

"What is it?"

"I've just seen a little lizard."

"Don't be daft. It's too cold for lizards."

"I'm looking at it *now*, and it's looking at me."

"You're not serious?"

But he was.

The lizard—a very small one—had squeezed itself up against the warm outer tiles of the hearth.

"Crikey," I said. "I thought you were kidding. How on earth did it get in here?"

"Shall I try and pick it up?" said Zach.

The lizard took a timid dart towards us and looked up at our faces.

"Hey, it wants to be friends."

It lifted up one of its front legs and kept darting its tongue in and out.

"Hey, look—it's trying to talk to us."

"Lizards always do that," I said.

"Come on, little lizard. Sometimes their tail comes off when you catch them," said Zach. The lizard backed off a bit then. We still hadn't caught it when the cat came in.

"I wonder if cats eat lizards," said Zach. "Kill!" he said, suddenly changing his tactics and pointing Whitey at the lizard. I don't know if she would have, she's a very dopey cat. Anyway, she didn't get a chance. The lizard flattened itself under the back door and shot outside.

"Aw," said Zach, "it might die now, in the cold. What shall I do?"

"Push off," I said, "and leave me in peace."

Time passed. I can't remember who first noticed Crispin was missing: I think it was Mum. Dad had just come back from the lab. He said "I expect he's upstairs; I'm going up, I'll have a look in his room." A few minutes later, he called down "He's not there."

"He hid from us this morning," said Lottie. "I'm not looking for him." But pretty soon she was helping the rest of us. We looked everywhere, but Crispin was nowhere to be found. Mum suddenly began to get anxious.

"It's so queer," she kept saying. "I mean, where can he be?" She sounded more and more tense. "Have you been nasty to him?"

We said no—not really.

"You don't think he's gone off outside somewhere, do you?" she said. "I mean, would he—by himself? A timid little boy like that?"

And Dad said: "If he's not inside, he must be outside."

"Oh, my God," Mum was nearly crying—"and it's already dark. I'll come with you."

"No, don't you come."

"He's not timid," said Zach, but no one took any notice.

"I must come with you. I'd go out of my mind waiting."

"All right," Dad agreed. "We'll need a flashlight."

Dad told us on no account to go out looking ourselves, but to start searching again at the top of the house, open every cupboard, look under every bed, etc. etc. "Oh—and try and think where you saw him last."

Then they went off to get warm clothes and electric torches.

"Come on, you," said Zach, to me.

"Shut up," I said. "I'm thinking. Dad told us to."

When did we last seem him? Or hear him?

WHEN DID I LAST HEAR HIM?

I ran into the kitchen. I looked behind the door. I looked for little holes in the skirting board by the fire, where it was warm. I'm a loony, I thought—the others were out looking for Crispin: I just wanted to find the lizard.

I opened the back door and a wedge of light shone out into the yard. I stood shivering and shaking in the night air.

The cat walked in.

"Oh, Whitey," I said. "You've not eaten him, have you?"

It crossed my mind, maybe I really was barmy. No of course not, I thought, I'm all right—still, perhaps all barmy people think they're all right. And then I thought: I didn't actually *see* anything happen to Crispin, and anyway, cats don't eat lizards, do they? And all the time I was thinking these daft thoughts I was looking for footprints in the snow—the sort little hands would make—but we'd shovelled a clear path to Timothy's stable and the coal shed, and there was nothing to see.

I heard someone come into the kitchen. It was Mrs. Korngold. I rushed back in.

"Oh, Mrs. Korngold," I said—I didn't give myself time to think—"please—you've got to help us. We want Crispin back."

"If he's lost," she said, "let him stay lost. Close the door."

"You don't understand. I know he's a pain in the neck, but if anything's happened to him it'll make my mother ill. Honestly it will."

"What do you expect me to do about it?"

"Just help us, *please*." Desperate as I was, I couldn't quite get out the words "change him back." There was something about Mrs. Korngold just then that made me afraid to. But as I watched, the crossness went out of her face.

"*Please*, before Mum and Dad go out looking."

"Oh, very well," she said at last. "You'll find him in the stable with the pony."

"Thanks!"

I skidded across the icy yard and switched on the stable light. Crispin was crawling sleepily out of a mound of straw. I rushed back in the house. Dad was just opening the front door.

"Wait!" I yelled. "I've found him!" And the next thing, we were all laughing because Timothy was pushing him gently into the kitchen with his nose. At the time, all the puzzlement got swallowed up in the relief. We were so glad to see him, nobody cared that Crispin couldn't explain why he was in the stable—or why we hadn't noticed him there before, because we had looked. Dad said he must be another absent-minded member of the family, like himself, Lottie said Timothy had found him, and wasn't he a clever pony? Crispin just went on sitting in the kitchen plucking straws out of his jumper and shuddering from time to time, and Mum served hot chocolate all round.

Of course now I *knew* there was something very queer going on in our house, and I expect you think I was pretty slow not to get on to it before. I knew that Mrs. Korngold was a strange and powerful being, besides being our home help. I knew it, and I did nothing about it. Why not? You'll have this hard to swallow—I knew it, but I still couldn't believe it.

What didn't occur to me was that other people might have started noticing strange things too …

Just to finish off about Crispin. He stayed on another week or so, but the fight had gone out of him and the rest of his visit was uneventful. I did ask him what happened that day in the kitchen, but it was no use. He couldn't remember. Once I caught him holding a dead moth that he found on a window ledge.

"What do you want that for?" I asked.

"I don't know," he said, with a dazed expression on his face. And for quite some time he had a strange habit of licking his lips with a quick dart of his tongue. (I wonder what his mother made of that?) For myself, I was surprised to find I was really quite glad about old Crispin, and not just Crispin, because I thought—if Crispin had returned to normal (normal?), the odds were that that traffic warden had too. You remember? The day we went shopping? … if he ever was a dog, that is … I was never entirely sure about that.

7

IN THE AFTERNOON of the day Crispin went home, Lottie, Zach and I were alone in Zach's bedroom. Lottie and I were reading by the window: it was a darkish afternoon, dull and gray outside. Zach was playing snakes and ladders against himself.

Lottie looked up and said, "Mrs. Korngold makes you see things that aren't there."

Zach stopped playing and I closed my book.

"How do you mean?" I said.

"Well," said Lottie, "you know that old cemetery near our school"—I should explain here that Lottie and one of her morbid little chums, not Theresa, another girl, like looking for old rhymes and old dates in churchyards. Some people collect train numbers; Lottie collects gravestones—"Well, I'd been playing around there after school," she said, "and when I came home I was thinking about it and feeling sad. I was sitting at the kitchen table and I started drawing a picture of the churchyard—not that Greek temple bit at the gate, but the old villagey part inside, with stone crosses and angels and all that. Anyway, I started feeling sadder and sadder, thinking about all the people being alive, you know, like we are now, and then being dead—like in that song about John

Peel: 'Now is he gone, far far away, with his hounds and his horn in the morning …'"

"Don't cry now, Lottie," I said.

She sort of gulped: "That song always makes me cry. Well, while I was looking at my picture and feeling sad …"

"Yes? Go on. We know you were feeling sad. What happened then?"

"Well, all the gravestones changed into dead leaves." She sat back and looked at us.

"What do you mean?"

She gave a sigh, as if we were very stupid. "There was a big tree in my picture, see, all black and bare like I saw it. Well, now it had green leaves on, and all the gravestones had turned into old leaves off this tree, colored ones. And I felt cheered up."

"Why?"

"I don't know."

"You've made me go all goosey," said Zach.

"What happened next?" I said. "Go on."

"That's it. Then they changed back again."

"Oh, is that all?" said Zach.

"You wouldn't say that if a picture you drew changed into something else while you were looking at it."

"How does Mrs. Korngold come into it?" I said.

"Oh, she was just there, sitting at the table with me."

"Perhaps you fell asleep," said Zach.

"No I didn't."

We pondered it over for a bit.

"I think Mrs. Korngold is a bit strange," I said cautiously. "I wonder where she comes from?"

We talked that over. It turned out that Lottie and I both had a fairly similar impression—you remember the picture I got when I opened the door to Mrs. Korngold, of Stukas dive-bombing, and the refugees with the hand-carts? Well, she got one too, not exactly the same as mine, but quite like it, not long after Mrs. Korngold came.

"Were there any boats in your picture?" Lottie asked.

I thought for a minute. "I'm not sure," I said, "but it's funny you should ask me that, because there was a sort of feel of the sea about it. You know, as if the sea wasn't far off …"

"I know what it was!" cried Lottie. "It sounds just like that film on Dunkirk that Mum made us watch on TV—the bit where the ordinary families were trying to get away to the coast."

She was right!

"Mine wasn't quite the same—there weren't any airplanes or ships: just people on each side of a high wall who wanted to get to each other—they kept reaching out their hands—only there were men with machine guns guarding the gate and stopping them."

"Checkpoint Charlie!" I said. "In the Berlin Wall—Dad's been through it. Don't you remember? He told us about it."

"I've seen it on an old News programme too, in black and white," said Lottie.

I said: "She drags thoughts you've got in the back of your head out to the front."

"Ugh." Lottie made a face. Her voice sank to a whisper. "Crikey, isn't it scary?"

She must have been scared because she'd forgotten to swear in French.

"I wonder if she can put thoughts in as well as drag them out …" At this point a faint warning bell seemed to sound in my head, but I ignored it and went on eagerly. "I say, do you remember when we were talking about Mrs. Slip Slop and she changed the way she walked? Come on, Zach—she talks to you more than us. Has she told you anything?"

"She doesn't really talk to me—she just tells me stories," said

Zach, in his normal foghorn tones.

"Hush!" we both said. Again I had that faint uneasy feeling.

We all froze for a moment, but there was nothing to hear.

"Listen, Zach," whispered Lottie, "have you ever seen a picture in your mind or anything that made you think you knew where Mrs. Korngold came from? We're trying to find out about her home."

It took us a while to make Zach understand what we were after, but at last he said: "Oh, yes, I remember. There were all these women in like long black fluttery clothes, sort of."

"Go on."

"Well, it's daft. They were screaming and ripping their clothes up worse. Oh yes, and there was a great big model of a horse behind them, and a city with towers all burning. I think she was one of them," he added vaguely.

It was my turn for the chill trickle up my spine. "Lumme—he's been looking at the Wooden Horse of Troy," I said.

"Oh, he's just muddled it up with a story," said Lottie crossly.

"No—don't you see?" I said. "They were all sad people, but different sad people—yours, mine, his. She took something out of our minds, that we'd already seen or heard—and used it …"

"It won't tell us anything, then," said Lottie. "If it's all just things we've seen before."

"I'm not sure. Just shut up a minute while I think. Look—they were all unhappy, in distress, not in their own homes where they really belonged …"

They kept quiet for a couple of seconds … but I wasn't getting anywhere.

"Oh, well, never mind that," said Lottie. "What I want to know is, do you think she's—a witch? She could be a white witch—you know—a good one," she added hastily.

"She's always good to us," I said. "And Mum. Mum likes her."

Then I remembered Crispin. She hadn't been good to him. I

opened my mouth to tell them, and felt again something within me urging me quite strongly not to. So I told myself that I wasn't one hundred per cent sure about it anyway, and that I wasn't out to frighten them; and I didn't mention him—I was scared to. I jumped up and switched on the light, and that made it seem better.

"No, Lottie," I said, "I don't think she's a witch."

"Do you think we ought to tell Mum?" said Zach.

"Yes, let's."

"No!"

Lottie and I spoke together.

"Why not?" she said. "It's a darn good idea."

"No," I said again, more quietly. "Mum's not well, and Dad said we musn't pester her. She's got enough to do."

It was quite true, as far as it went. She did have a load of work on, and Beth to mind, and if she wasn't exactly sick she wasn't her usual bouncing self either.

"We could say something to Dad," said Lottie, but she didn't sound madly enthusiastic.

"Don't you think he'll say we're silly, or it's all in our own minds, or something?" I said. "We've got to have something definite to show, some proof."

"My picture was definite," said Lottie.

"More definite than that … I mean, where is it now?" I argued reasonably.

We went on a bit longer like that, back and forth and so on—but in the end the poor little mutts swallowed it, though not without a fight, and I had to compromise a bit.

"O.K.," I agreed. "Just one more thing, and we tell—one more queer thing of any kind, whether we've got any proof or not."

"O.K.," said Lottie, "and I'm going to keep a jolly good watch out."

"And so am I," said Zach.

They probably thought we were all being extremely sensible—I mean, I'm supposed to be the sensible one. Me? Sensible? Do you know why I really didn't want them to tell? I'd had a dream. Not a funny sort of half-dream like the night of the storm: this time I'd been properly asleep in bed. In fact I'd forgotten all about it till the moment I'd shouted "No!", and then it came back to me, warning and all.

It was like something that once really happened. We were on holiday in Cornwall. I'll tell you the real thing first, though I'm not sure if I truly remember it or it's just that I've heard it told so often—you know how it is. I was about four, and Lottie was just a baby—a cross one—in a little buggy. Mum took us for a walk along a cliff path. It seemed quite safe. There was healthy grass on one side and a low stone wall on the other, with another few yards of turf beyond it before the cliff fell away to the sea. I climbed up on the wall. I remember I had tartan gym-shoes with "left foot", "right foot" written on them, and some green dungarees from Sears Roebuck, so stiff they stood up by themselves. The path started to dip down, but the wall got higher, much higher. I walked along admiring my shoes, and slowly getting ahead of Mum and Lottie. Then Lottie got her foot stuck in the wheel of the push-chair and started to cry. Mum had to stop and sort her out.

"Adam," she called, "is there still some ground between you and that sea?"

I looked at where the grass ought to be. There was no grass: the cliff face fell sheer, three hundred feet below me. Great green waves boiled in over jagged rocks. I can hear them booming now if I think about it. Mum must have glanced up, seen me frozen there, and looked for herself. I had three yards to go before the turf began again. She started talking to me, quite calmly and not too loud.

"My—you *have* balanced well," she said. "Now just keep on walking slowly, and don't look down. That's right. You can watch where you put your feet, but *don't look down.*" Her voice was getting nearer … "Would you like to give me your hand?" She reached up, grasped it, grabbed me—and I was safely down. Okay, she saved me from falling, but the real point was, the ground had been sheared off *for the last fifteen feet.* I'd already walked nearly five yards in perfect safety, *because I hadn't noticed the danger.* (I might have seen it out of the corner of my eye, but I hadn't really noticed.) Dad said after: "Some dangers you look in the eye: with others, better you carry on as if they weren't there."

In my dream it all looked a bit different, but I knew it for the same place—green hills, a fishing village, and a rocky coast. There was sea on both sides in my dream, and the stones of the wall were wet. Mum was ahead, holding out her hand to me, only it wasn't really her, because I suddenly saw she had the face of Mrs. Korngold, and somehow the whole family was behind me, Mum and Dad too. It was all about ten thousand times ghastlier than it was in real life, with the waves crawling sickeningly over the rocks and the awful fear of falling, but Mrs. Korngold went on holding out her hand and I knew in the dream I must trust her, like I'd trusted Mum.

Ignore the danger; act as if you didn't know—and don't gang up on her: that was the warning I had in my dream.

Of course, after all that, nothing happened for ages—except that the winter got worse and there was more snow, more power cuts, and more difficulties over food and fuel, till Dad said it was worse than bally wartime. We were glad we hadn't bothered Mum. She really wasn't all that well, she seemed to get one cold after another, though Beth, by the way, was flourishing. Mrs. Korngold looked after her quite a lot. It was just Mum who seemed at a low ebb. She said herself that if she was a motor-bike she could be described as running on her reserve tank. As for Lottie, Zach and me, we just jogged on a day at a time, home and school, school and home—but as I look back on it now it was as if we were holding our breath, waiting for the next thing.

8

JUST BEFORE CHRISTMAS Lottie had her tenth birthday: she didn't get a lot, because it was costing a bomb to buy hay for Timothy. Actually, judging by the presents, there was some doubt whether it was his birthday of hers: e.g. Zach's present was a bunch of carrots and I gave her a thing called a dandy brush which is a sort of horse's hair-brush. As a matter of fact she did get something for herself: a tweed hacking jacket, second-hand, but very nice, from the parents, and a big parcel of pony books, fact and fiction, new and old, from Aunt Cecilia who used to be mad on horses herself when young. She didn't have a party, but Theresa and another girl, called Marion (the one she went round the graveyard with), came to tea. Mrs. Korngold had laid on a lavish spread with luscious fresh peaches—we'd no idea where she got them from—as her present.

Christmas went by rather quietly with Mum not being so well, but we did go to one party, at the stately home. Blodgett Hall really did look like the Winter Palace now, with snow on all the window ledges and icicles hanging off the porch. The party didn't go on very long, as the weather was now so bitter cold, and everyone was really better off at home. Everything was frozen and dead. I suppose it was quite pretty to look at, like Christmas cards and scenes from Dickens, but murder if you went out in it. After a bit it got you down, always being cold. Animals and birds suffered too. We saw all sorts of tracks near the house every morning in the snow, and sometimes we caught a glimpse of the animals themselves: deer, foxes, squirrels, a white stoat once, and even a badger. We put out food and water for the birds, but it was never long before the water froze over. One morning we noticed more animal tracks than ever. I'd just taken a tray of tea upstairs for Mum. Dad was having a cup of tea with her before his breakfast, and Mum was staying in bed with yet another cold and a bit of a temperature. She had her bed by the window, with a nice view out into the orchard, and her work spread out on the bedside table.

"I expect they're after Timothy's food," I said—you could see tracks all through the orchard.

"Seems as if the wild things like us," said Dad.

"Hm—I'm not sure if I like the wild things," said Mum. "Look, on the small apple tree—isn't that an owl? That's not a bird I like to see in daylight. It's spooky."

"It's only a 'little owl'," said Dad. "I'm not too keen myself on barn owls—you know, the big ones that fly absolutely silently. They'd give anyone the creeps."

"It's the little ones I don't like," said Mum. "They're an omen of death. All right, you can smile, but the night my grandfather died in Boston a little owl screeched all night in a park across the road."

"Mrs. Bramble!" Mrs. Korngold's voice sounded from below.

"Oh, I forgot," I said. "She asked me to tell you not to be long, Dad—she's cooking you some liver."

"I suppose I'd better go," he said with a sigh. "Not that I'm in any hurry to see my dear colleague Dr. Daniels this morning. Honestly, that man drives me up the pole …"

"*Don't!*" interrupted Mum.

"Don't what?"

"Don't mention anything to Mrs. Korngold about him! … I just thought you might," she added feebly. "When you go down, I mean."

He looked at her, surprised. She had sounded almost scared. "All right, love. Don't fret: I wasn't going to. You're a bit jumpy, aren't you? You just stay there and take life easy. I'll see you before I go."

Dad went down, and I waited for Mum to finish her tea. She does actually quite like tea, despite that time she chucked it on the kitchen floor. But she stopped in mid-gulp.

"Gee!" she said. "What is she doing now with that blood?"

I went and looked too. Mrs. Korngold had come into the orchard and scraped a place clear of snow with her shoe. In her hand she had a white plastic butcher's tray out of the fridge, slopping over with blood. You get a lot of blood out of liver.

"I guess she's going to put it on the fruit trees or something; I believe it does them good—or is it roses?"

"The cat likes it," I said.

"Well, run down and tell her," said Mum, with something of her old firm manner.

I didn't go. It was too late anyway—she was already pouring it into the ground, slowly.

"You'd better tell her another time not to do that, and give it to Whitey," Mum said.

I hesitated. "Don't you think she looks as if she's saying her prayers, or something?" I caught Mum's eye, but in a moment she looked away.

"Mrs. Korngold does some very strange things," she said. "I wouldn't say I had her quite figured out."

"Mum …" I began.

"Hush a minute."

Mrs. Korngold had turned round to come in the house. For a moment though she stood looking up at the sky. Her face was so utterly woebegone, we drew back from the window, ashamed somehow to be staring at her. Mum said in a whisper "What do you make of that?" Then she pulled herself together. "Adam—I don't want you to get involved. Don't say anything to her about the blood, and don't worry—I can cope with Mrs. Korngold—only not just now."

"But Mum …"

"Put it out of your head—I mean that. And here—you can take this tea-tray downstairs. Hurry up, you'll be late for school."

I went downstairs, quite a bit cheered up. She knew, the same as we did, that our home help was—different. We weren't on our own anymore. I got ready for school.

By this time—it was February—we were about two weeks into the Spring term. Spring! Some hopes. The roads were still being salted, and there were banks of snow in all the gutters. I still got to school most days, but Mum didn't always send Zach or Lottie, because of the cold. Imagine my surprise, then—the weather being what it was—when I arrived home a day or two later to find a hiker, or a climber or someone, with boots and a rucksack anyway, knocking at our back door. He was incredibly healthy-looking—he was actually sun-tanned—and he was tall, with blue eyes and crinkly gold hair showing under his woolly cap; very pale hair, almost silver, and he was wearing all this sort of climbing gear. Come to think of it, he didn't look quite like an ordinary climber, because on top of his woolly jumper and so on he had black overalls, and a very thick leather belt round his middle.

First he asked if we could spare him a drop of milk—he thought our house was a farm, so he said. I told him it wasn't, but I asked him in and offered him a cup of tea. He came in and took off his cap, and sat down at the table—I swear, even his hair looked extra healthy. Lottie and Zach were in the kitchen on their own making a jigsaw puzzle. The kettle was boiling and I brewed up. I make a mean cup of tea.

"Where's Mrs. Korngold?" I asked.

"Dunno," said Zach. "Haven't seen her for a bit."

"Mrs. Korngold?" said our visitor. "Is that the rather large lady with fair hair?"

"Yes, that's right. Do you know her?"

"I think I've seen her about," he said vaguely. "Er … I wonder if I could possibly have a word with her?"

What on earth for, I thought. Of course, I didn't say that. I just told Zach to go and look for her.

"O.K.," said Zach. He got down from the table slowly, falling over the visitor's boots. They were pretty huge. "Have you been climbing in this weather?" he asked.

The man laughed. "Oh, I don't go up, I go down, underground. The climate down there doesn't change. It's called potholing—have you heard of it?"

"No," said Zach. "What is it?"

"You go underground—they drop you, actually, on the end of a rope—and you can explore caves and subterranean rivers … and other places. Sometimes," he went on quickly, "it's so narrow you have to crouch down and wriggle through, and you can feel the rock on every side. When it's really tight you can hear your own heart magnified, beating back at you from the passage walls. Other times you come out into great caverns, so high your light scarcely reaches the roof, and if your light goes out all you sense round you is—nothingness."

"Crikey," said Zach. "I wouldn't fancy that."

Lottie went a delicate shade of pale green. For a minute she looked scared stiff.

"Go on, hop it," I said to Zach. "See if you can find Mrs. Korngold."

"O.K., *bwana*." He stopped, leaving the door half open, and sending a freezing draft round our ankles. "Who shall I say wants her?"

"You can tell her my name's … Swift," said the potholer. "That's it—Swift."

Funny fellow, I thought. He sounded for all the world as if he'd just made it up that minute.

"Swift by name and swift by nature," he blurbed on—he seemed pleased with himself. "She'll know. Dick Swift."

Zach pushed off into the hall, banging the door behind him. Lottie, who had bucked up again and had been staring rather rudely at our visitor, suddenly asked: "Did you come here before, once? Our Mum and Dad gave a party, a bit since, and I was wondering if I'd seen you before."

"Oh. Let me see," said the potholer. Er—yes. That is to say—no. I'm not sure—I can't remember. Ah, thank you, Adam, a cup of tea, lovely—thank you very much."

He knew my name.

While he drank Lottie got up and started making very obvious signals to me and mouthing "He *was* here."

I didn't quite know what to do.

"How do you see, underground?" said Lottie, still sounding very hostile. "Do you carry a torch or something?"

"When I'm going down I have to put on a helmet with a lamp in it. That's what my belt's for, to hold a battery and an electric lead."

He was still showing us how he attached the various bits of himself when Zach came back and said, "It's funny, I can't find

PATRICIA MILES

Mrs. Korngold anywhere. Mum says would you like to talk to her instead, Mr.-er-Swift?"

"No, no thanks," said Mr. Swift. "Never mind. Lovely cup of tea, thanks again. Perhaps I'll drop by later." He took himself off then, pretty quick.

"I didn't think much of him," said Lottie. "Sneaky thing. He jolly well was here: not in those clothes, though. Are you sure you didn't see him, Adam?"

I shook my head. And yet I did feel there was something familiar about him. But I couldn't quite place it.

Lottie gave a little shiver. "That what he said about those underground caves—some of it was like my dream. You know, when I fell off Timothy. There were bits of my dream I'd forgotten. That nothingness bit. Ugh—he gave me the creeps."

A few minutes later Mrs. Korngold came into the kitchen: she must have been in the house all the time, because she didn't have her outdoor clothes on. We told her about Mr. Swift.

"Him!" she snorted. "That's the second time he's been around today. Don't ask him in if he comes again. Tell him I'm out. I don't want to see him." She was very emphatic.

"Curiouser and curiouser," said Lottie to me under her breath, the aloud: "He certainly was an awful liar."

"He told us he'd been potholing," said Zach, "under the ground."

But Mrs. Korngold was not to be drawn about Mr. Swift.

"Did he indeed?" she said, in the sort of tone that warned us to drop the subject. The conversation turned to other things.

Afterwards, as soon as Lottie and I were alone, she grabbed my arm and said in a phony sort of doom-laden voice: "Adam, I bet it's all going to start up again. Funny things will happen."

"Why? What makes you say that?"

"I dunno, I guess I just have a feeling about it," she said darkly.

I scoffed. My mother and sister sometimes go in for having "feelings" about things. They reckon they've got extra-sensory perception and telepathic powers and all that. (They also read their fortunes in magazines.) Abso-bally-lutely daft, Dad says. But I just mention it, in the cause of science, in case *you* ever come up against feminine intuition. For what it's worth—and it's an isolated case no doubt—we only had to wait that one night before Lottie and her bally "feeling" were proved … well, you'll see.

The next day was a Wednesday, my half-day at school. I'd got an interesting afternoon planned for myself: I'd been getting on with my map of the wild garden, showing all the footpaths and grottoes and everything (it was jolly good—all in color), but I needed to go up there and check some of the detail, and there was still quite a large area to explore. Meanwhile, there was morning school toget through.

It began all right with Assembly followed by double History. We were near the end of the first period, with our hands just about dropping off from taking notes, when someone showed up at the outside windows of the classroom and rapped on the snowy glass. We all looked round. I got a shock. It was our potholer, woolly hat and all. Mr. Cosgrove, our teacher, flapped his hands at him to make him go away. He didn't go away. Mr. Cosgrove looked crossly along the front row and his eye happened to light on me. (I say "happened," though afterwards it was quite clear that nothing that morning really happened by chance.) "Bramble," he said, "tell him to go round to the main entrance, whatever he wants."

"Yes, sir." My mind was churning, thanks to Lottie's suspicious mind. What on earth was he doing here, what could he want? I was going slowly up the aisle between the desks, worrying, tripping over briefcases and so on—when it hit me. I remembered. His voice! It was his voice that had been familiar. His was the man's voice we'd heard arguing with Mrs. Korngold—through the kitchen door, the night of Mum's party, the night of the first power cut.

"Hurry up, Bramble!" said Mr.. Cosgrove.

I started a protracted struggle with the window.

"What's the matter with you, lad?"

"It's my hand, sir. It's weak from taking notes."

"And no doubt the same applies to your head. Get on with it."

General cries of "My hand aches, too, sir" "My hand's dropping off," etc. Then the window came open with a crunch from all the ice in the crevices.

"If you want to see the headmaster ..." I mumbled.

"It's you I want to see," said Mr. Swift pleasantly.

If Mrs. Korngold didn't want to see him, I sure as hell didn't either. A wave of panic hit me.

"Me?"

Whatever he wanted to say, I didn't want to hear. But I didn't know how to block him off like Mrs. Korngold, or disappear. Disappear? Had she, yesterday afternoon? I didn't have time to work that one out. All I could do was stand well back, blurt out Mr. Cosgrove's message, carefully avoiding Mr. Swift's eye, and dash back to my seat. I left the window for someone else to close. I sat down, and then Rumbold put his hand up. "Please sir, is that right, what you've got on the blackboard?"

"Of course, it's right." Mr. Cosgrove turned round and had a look. "Good heavens." He read: "'Christopher Columbus discovered China in 1492.' *China?* How on earth did I come to write that?"

"That's funny sir," said our history whiz-kid, one Tweeting by name. "It was all right before. I've got 'America' where it says 'China' now, and I copied it off the board." (Cries of "Smart Alec," "You would have," etc.) Oddly enough, I thought it had said "America" before. I just had to take a quick glance over my shoulder: Dick Swift was still there, grinning. He winked at me, then walked away. He looked friendly enough but I found my heart was thumping.

A few minutes later we had another distraction—this time in the shape of a window-cleaner—and I didn't choose that expression, "in the shape," lightly. We have a wooden partition that divides the classroom from the corridor. He came rattling along and put his ladder up against the partition. He was a big, heavy-faced man in white overalls and he fairly punished the windows, leaning on them hard and making them rattle. He started whistling as he worked. Mr. Cosgrove turned round in irritation and the whole class looked up. The man stopped whistling and gave an apologetic shrug. Then, while I was still looking, *he sort of shimmered and changed before my eyes.* It was him again—the potholer, Dick Swift! It was over in a moment. He just permitted me a split-second glimpse of the inner window-cleaner, so to speak, then he resumed his outer shape. For a moment I was paralyzed, eyes sticking out like organ stops, jaw hanging open, etc. Then I shook Rumbold by the arm in a frenzy. "Hey—did you see that?"

"What? Leave go. What do you think you're doing?"

"Never mind," I groaned.

"Look what you've made me do—I've smudged my book."

"Sorry."

I put my head down and willed myself not to look up again from my desk. I didn't even look at the blackboard, I just copied from Rumbold, not a good idea as a rule. After a while I heard the bucket go clanking away down the corridor. I risked a quick glance. He had gone.

At break, which we have early on Wednesdays, I stuck like a leech to Rumbold and a couple of other pals of ours. It was too cold to go out, and the school provided a thick dense mass of protective cover, viz. a mob of boys. Their own mothers would have had a job to pick out their offspring in a mass like that, all milling about in the same uniform. I felt safe enough till the bell went.

After break it was time for one of our memorable sessions with Mr. Busby. He surged in, looking as usual as if he had just drunk a gallon or two of the elixir of life, black bushy beard wagging, black gown floating out behind. Count Dracula in person. (Did I tell you the teachers still wear gowns at this school?) While everyone else was shaking in their shoes I actually felt a mild sense of relief. I didn't see how anyone could get at me in Mr. Busby's lesson.

We all stood up, looking as well-behaved and intelligent as possible.

"Good morning, boys," he boomed. "We're going to do some experiments with heat this morning. I'm going to demonstrate violent reactions." (Appropriate, I thought.) "We'll go up to the lab. QUIETLY! Just bring your notebooks."

We filed meekly out.

When we got to the lab an electrician, a thin dark chap, was fiddling about with the light switch.

"This won't take long, sir," he said respectfully. "Shall I finish it now, or would you like me to come back later?"

"What's the matter with it?"

For answer the electrician pressed down the switch: a brilliant blue flash flew out of the wall, two bulbs burst, and there was a loud bang. We'd have cheered if it had been any other teacher.

Mr. Busby let out a laugh like three lorries changing gear and three metal rods at the back of the lab started to vibrate on the same note; he said, "I think you'd better finish it now."

"Thank you, sir,"—and the "electrician" turned and gave me a sly smile.

Oh lumme. I dived into the middle of the front bench, next to swotty old Trubshaw, and right under Mr. Busby's nose.

"What are you doing, Bramble?" said Mr. Busby sharply.

"Sorry, sir. I wanted to be near the experiment."

"Crawler," muttered Hillier on my right. I kicked him on the ankle, red-headed rugby-playing oaf. Despite myself my eyes slid in the direction of our electrician. Maybe I was mistaken … Not on your life. Need I tell you? Yes, it was Mr. Swift again.

I wished he wouldn't do that—keep flashing me the inner golden-haired healthy type, I mean. Every time he did it it gave me this quaking feeling in the chest. Like if a mouse darts across the floor—it doesn't actually do anything to you, but it moves so fast it makes you jump. I knew it was absolutely useless, but I just couldn't stop myself actually rubbing my eyes.

"… WELL, BRAMBLE! I'm waiting. What's the matter with you, boy? Are you dreaming?"

Oh, crumbs. Mr. Busby had asked me something and I hadn't been listening. You never get a minute's peace in Mr. Busby's lessons; while he's assembling stuff for one experiment, he's throwing out questions at you on something else you're supposed to have learned before.

"Tell him, Hillier. Come on, come on: what you know already about heat—three ways by which heat travels."

"Er, yes sir. Er: conduction … convection … and er …" (gasp of relief) "radiation, sir."

"I'm surprised you don't know that, Bramble."

Well I did, of course. That was the maddening thing. He struck a match to light the bunsen burner on the teacher's bench and inspiration hit me—a red herring so succulent Mr. Busby was sure to fall for it, unless of course the presence of Mr. Swift put him off. Some teachers don't act natural when there's an outsider in the classroom.

Still—if only I dared … I might become famous in the school for ever … it was worth a try.

"Er, I was just wondering, sir … isn't heat, I mean fire, one of the four things people thought the world was made of? In the olden days, I mean?"

Mr. Busby jerked his head up, surprised.

"'Elements,' lad, not 'things.' Mm." He looked thoughtfully at some cottonwool and a jar of white stuff he'd put out on the bench, decided to ignore them and went on. "An interesting question of yours, Bramble. Earth, air, fire and water—that's what they thought the world was made of … That was an idea of the Greeks. The same notion was taken up later by the alchemists …" A dreamy look crossed his face, as if he could hear beautiful music playing. Hillier kicked me back excitedly in the ankle: we held our breath.

"The quest of the alchemists," intoned Mr. Busby. "Fascinating. Chemistry plus magic. A search for the fundamental stuff the universe was made of. Actually, in the end they thought it was something they called essence of mercury. I suppose we could just take a look at mercury …"

He was off! Good old Busby! I should have known. If a troop of baboons had come in to hang up Christmas decorations it wouldn't have bothered him. In fact, far from the intruder influencing Mr. Busby, it was the other way round. I don't know if you've ever been in school when the decorators or window-cleaners are in, and gradually they stop working and start taking an interest in the lesson—well, it was like that with our electrician. First of all he swept up the glass from the shattered bulbs, very, very slowly. Then he fixed it that half the lights came on, but he still didn't go.

He just hung about, pretending to do something to a wall plug.

Mr. Busby interrupted himself and said "Is that all the light we're going to get?"

"For the moment, sir," replied the electrician.

Mr. Busby seemed pleased. "Well, it's too dark for you to write. Close up your notebooks. Perhaps we might allow ourselves a few distractions … Let me see. I intended to give you a lesson on violent reactions this morning—as a warning to you to be careful … I think I can relate that to the topic of alchemy—in which as you may know I am interested—quite instructively, so as to stop you lot BLOWING YOURSELVES UP: not in my lab, anyway. So—let us follow up Bramble's red herring, so to speak, and see what we can find out."

He rubbed his hands and beamed round the dim lab. I'm not sure Mr. Busby in a good mood wasn't more alarming than his ordinary self. Different, anyway.

"Strictly speaking," he said, "this topic belongs not to science as we know it, but to the history of science. Have I your attention?"

He had.

"Let's look at mercury, then," said Mr. Busby, selecting a jar from the glass-fronted cupboard near the blackboard. "Mysterious stuff. The only liquid metal."

Mr. Swift stopped all pretence of work and turned round openly to watch.

"Mercury," continued Mr. Busby. "Very dangerous, expensive, gives off poisonous fumes. Sniff too much and your hair falls out. Nasty, treacherous stuff."

Crikey. Something was wrong. I sensed a powerful blast of emotion from the "electrician"—and if you think I was getting extra sensitive, well, next to me even Hillier shuddered, and he hadn't a clue what was going on.

"Look at it," Mr. Busby went on. He poured some into a flat dish: it rolled itself into little balls and ran about. "Here, there and everywhere: quick and unreliable—called after the Roman god of trickery and cunning; he conducted the souls of the dead—an unpleasant fellow."

There *was* something Mr. Swift didn't like, I didn't know what. Maybe it was something Mr. Busby had said. Ought I to warn him? I could just see myself standing up and saying "… er, excuse me, sir, but I think the electrician isn't … er … human. He's supernatural, sir. Could be hostile. I think he's something to do with a lady who works in our house and *she* changed my cousin into a lizard ...""

There are some things you just can't say—not unless you want to get put away in a comfortable locked room somewhere.

"Now why were they interested in mercury?" continued Mr. Busby happily. "Well, they thought they could work wonders with it. They were looking for something that would—one: cure disease; two: restore youth; three: prolong life, and four: above all, turn lead into gold."

At this point he stopped and put a lump of lead, about the size and shape of a large block of chocolate, on the bench.

"They thought that if they could refine the four elements out of the mercury—earth, air, fire and water—what was left would have the power to transmute base metals into precious ones. Surprisingly enough they did succeed in reducing the mercury to a white powder—possibly it was this."

He got out another jar of stuff and unscrewed the lid. "This is mercuric thiocyanate." He sprinkled a little on the lead bar. "If we add a little white sulfur the lead bar will turn into silver—or shall we change it into gold? Why not? We just take a little of this red sulfur ... just a pinch will do ... so." He sprinkled that on top of the mercury thio-whatsit, then pushed the bar carelessly to one side.

"Well, of course, their thinking was nonsense, but their experimental work, refining, evaporating, condensing and so on, was extremely clever and the beginning of chemistry as we know it. And it's easy to see how chemistry could shade into conjuring and trickery. Why, even today we can produce some pretty queer effects ... like this ..."

He reached down another jar with something dark red in it. I thought for a minute it was blood.

"This is bromine," said Mr. Busby, "not discovered till 1836: but this will show you the almost magical properties some chemicals seem to have. We pour a very small amount into a beaker, and heat it up, so …"

He held it over the bunsen burner and in a few moments a weird-looking red gas started to crawl up the beaker. He put it in a stand. The gas crawled over the top and down the side.

"Yes, well—we know now why that is happening—bromine happens to be a gas which is much heavier than air. But imagine if you saw that back in the early days of science, because that is what alchemy belongs to: the alchemists were the precursors of our modern analytical chemists." He gazed fondly at the bromine. "Odd, stuff, isn't it? … Let's try something else, even more magical. How to get fire without using any kind of lighter. This brings me to what I was originally going to show you this morning—an AWFUL WARNING to be careful with quantities. We take a small ball of cottonwool"—he took one and put it on a tripod—"sprinkle a little of this creamy white solid on it—which is sodium peroxide—and now watch carefully: I take ONE DROP of water, which I add to the cottonwool—so …!"

Yikes! A great tongue of flame shot into the air and licked the ceiling. We all leapt about a foot off the ground, and so did Mr. Busby. The flame died down. I thought he looked a bit shaken, but he pulled himself together and said "How much water did I use, Trubshaw?"

"One drop, sir."

"Yes … well, let that be a lesson to you."

He ran his hand surreptitiously over his eyebrows, to see if they were still there, I suppose.

Our eyes recovered from the flash, and Mr. Busby's attention returned to the jar of white mercury powder still standing on the bench next to the lead brick.

"Of course!—a thing I'd forgotten—what you *can* do with this, and it's a pretty old-fashioned trick … we trickle some powder across the bench, so. Touch a match to it … and … watch closely …"

We watched all right. The powder swelled and started to move: it coiled and crawled like a snake of gray ash! It was marvelous; it was horrible.

"They're called Pharaoh's serpents. They used to be quite popular at one time …"

He made a few more—and while he was speaking and demonstrating, the bromine went on seeping over the edge of the glass, down the side, along the bench, and on to the floor. It was beginning to look like fog in a horror movie. Mr. Busby hadn't noticed, but should it be doing that?

I took a furtive glance sideways. What I can only describe as an evil smile was playing about the features of Dick Swift. He wiped it off and gave me an innocent stare. I wondered—with a flutter of hope—was he just *playing* with us, with me? Just playing to amuse himself? And I was getting ready to feel less frightened when suddenly the few lights that were working went out again and something very odd happened to the bromine.

Gosh, I wish I could show you what happened. I wish you could have seen our lab that wintry morning—I bet you've got nothing like it: no lights, except from the bunsen burner, dark old-fashioned benches, glass-fronted cupboards full of chemicals in jars, white faces of boys in the gloom—whitish, anyway. It was like a wizard's cave. The bromine was swirling round our ankles now in thick red clouds that were changing shape, changing into something, putting out feet and claws! They were like red dragons coming after us. A boy called Duckworth let out a shriek and climbed up on his stool. Hillier bounded away from groping red jaws, up one side of the lab and down the other.

At the same time the Pharaoh's serpents got out of hand. They went wriggling along the bench, one after the other, getting bigger and bigger. Shrieks on all sides, and a mad scramble to get on the top of the benches.

As for Mr. Busby, he was no use at all. His lead brick! What had happened to it? He was staring at it transfixed. He couldn't take his eyes off it. In the feeble rays of the bunsen burner it shone yellow. The lead had turned to gold.

He put out a shaking hand to touch it—and the lights came on. A blaze of light, it seemed, after the gloom.

The lead was lead again, Pharaoh's serpents stopped wriggling, and the red dragons—just disappeared. The bell rang.

"I don't think you'll have any more trouble now, sir," said the electrician. He picked up his tools, treated us all to a sardonic grin, and pushed off.

Mr. Busby ran his hands through his hair in a dazed way, then he straightened up and more or less visibly pulled himself together.

"I'm afraid I didn't quite cover all the points I intended to make this morning, but I hope I've aroused your interest in … er … spontaneous combustion and the beginnings of chemistry," he said. Shaken maybe, but professional to the last. "Good morning, boys. You may go."

"It was something to do with the lights," said Rumbold when we got outside.

Hillier said: "He's given that lesson to everyone in the school at some time or other. My brother told me, he's in the Sixth."

"I bet it wasn't as good as the lesson we had," said someone else.

"I wonder how he does the special effects?" said Trubshaw.

"My brother says he's a jolly good teacher"—Hillier again.

And so on and so forth. But it was Rumbold who had the last word. "Ah—if only *all* science lessons were like that!"

After this English came as something of an anticlimax, to begin with anyway. Our teacher was Mr. Greene, a nice enough bloke, young and enthusiastic and all that. He has red curly hair and is liable to short explosions of rage, but is basically friendly and not much of a disciplinarian, as he has poetry on the brain. He's always going on about Truth and Beauty and stuff like that, and is easily distracted. So we relaxed a bit. Also, it was the last lesson of the morning. In he breezed in old corduroys, red tie and red socks (that seem to be a sort of English teacher's uniform—anyway they all wear it) with a battered poetry book under his arm. We said "Good morning, sir," and he flung himself carelessly into his chair and ripped yet another six-inch tear into his gown.

"What would you like to do this morning?" he said. "'Kubla Khan'? Or 'Nutting'?"

It was too good to be true. "'Nutting,' sir, please sir, we'd like to do 'Nutting'! (= "nothing," get it?)—joyful shouts from all over the class. In the middle of this uproar a short thick-set man came into the classroom wearing a blue boiler suit and carrying a bag—*guess who?*

"Maintenance—come to fix the heating, sir. Won't disturb you." He went quietly to the back of the class and began taking out his tools.

Mr. Greene ran his fingers through his hair in a harassed way, had a short paroxysm of yelling at us, and then settled us down to a quite interesting introduction to "Kubla Khan," nice gory stuff about drugs and violence (all about how this bloke was really spelled Qubilai Khan and conquered the whole of Asia in about 1250, and how Coleridge took opium for his toothache and dreamt the whole poem, and about the man from Porlock who interrupted him when he was still in the middle of writing it down, and so he forgot the rest). Then Mr. Greene told us to empty our minds (no problem there) and just listen to the poem. It began all right—perhaps you know it:

In Xanadu did Kubla Khan
A stately pleasure-dome decree, etc.

He had the book, but he was saying it off by heart, with his eyes half shut. Then he got to a bit that went like this:

And from this chasm, with ceaseless turmoil seething,

As if this earth in short thick pants were breathing …

He opened his eyes in alarm and looked at the book. "Er—'fast thick pants,'" he said quickly. But the thick pants had done for him. We all burst out laughing and general merriment set in for about five minutes. Two people started punching each other up on the back row, and a few paper darts flashed round the room. One landed on my desk.

Hardly knowing I was doing it, I picked up the dart and threw it back. I swear it changed direction in mid-air. It went straight for Mr. Greene and hit him in the eye. Even for Mr. Greene this was too much.

"Get out, Bramble! Stand outside the door!"

"Yes sir. I'm sorry, sir." I started to trail slowly out.

"All finished now, sir," said the maintenance man. "Just got to pack up."

Oh lumme. Now he'd get me on my own.

"Hurry up, Bramble!" I slunk out. I heard the laughter begin to die down in the classroom—except for Rumbold, who was still killing himself.

"Outside the door, you too," roared Mr. Greene.

Hooray! Good old Mr. Greene—the only master in the school daft enough to send two boys out at the same time.

The "maintenance man" gave me a thoughtful look as he passed by us and went off down the corridor with his bag of tools.

Things quietened down in the classroom, and we were called back in.

The poem was quite good at the end:

> Beware! Beware!
> His flashing eyes, his floating hair!
> For he on honeydew hath fed
> And drunk the milk of paradise.

Just like Mr. Greene, especially that bit about his floating eyes and his flashing hair.

It was almost noon when one of the secretaries put her hand round the door. "Sorry to interrupt, Mr. Greene. Could you spare—er"—she looked at a card in her hand—"Bramble for a few minutes? Adam Bramble?"

Oh, *no*, I thought. Why can't he leave me alone?

"It's for his eye test. He missed it when the main batch were done at the beginning of the year."

It sounded so plausible. It didn't fool me, but what could I do? "Please sir, my mother's going to have me done privately," I lied.

Mr. Greene ignored me. "Take him and welcome," he said courteously to the secretary. And to me: "Don't hurry back."

She led me away. As we walked along the corridor the old nerve was hopping in my leg again. I remember wishing dully I could detect something more useful with it, like water or oil, not just situations of imminent danger: any fool can spot those.

The potholer—I still thought of him as that—was waiting for me in the little room next to the secretaries' office. This time he was appearing as a small gray-haired man with gold-rimmed specs: he'd put on a white coat, and had hung a chart with letters on it on the wall. But it was him all right—I got the usual quick glimpse.

"Eyesight been troubling you at all lately?" he said. "Any odd visual sensations?" Oh boy, he was a real joker. "Sit down, just a form to fill in first …" The secretary shut the door. He made a comic grimace and shrugged, like one who had extracted all the enjoyment he reasonably can from a situation and must now get down to business. Then he pushed a piece of paper across to me.

I looked down at the form—it wasn't anything to do with eye tests, it was one of those telegraph forms you see on the counters of Post Offices. I read:

REQUEST REGARDING RELATIVE GRANTED. STOP. EXPECT RETURN TOMORROW OR NEXT DAY. STOP. STAY INDEFINITE SUBJECT USUAL CONDITIONS REGARDING FOOD. STOP.

"What is it?"

He smiled. "It isn't for you. It's for Mrs. Korngold. I seem to be having some difficulty getting a message through to her. I don't think she realizes it's good news. Will you please see she gets it?"

I was so surprised and nervous I couldn't quite grasp that he'd finished with me. I didn't want to talk to him, but I couldn't help blurting out: "Is … is that all, sir?"

"That's all. Off you go."

Boy! What a relief! I went towards the door. Then, I still felt horribly talkative, so I asked him: "It's about her daughter, isn't it?"

"Her daughter? Oh, she's told you."

"Well, not much."

Suddenly I remembered what Lottie had seen in her mind when Mrs. Korngold first came—Checkpoint Charlie, and the Berlin

Wall. That fitted in, surely?

"Is she … is she coming from behind the Iron Curtain?"

He looked startled. "In a way. Something like that."

"Who shall I say sent it, sir?" Cunning, this.

He hesitated. "You don't know who I am?"

"No, sir. Well, I know your name's Mr. Swift; you told us. But … well, no sir."

He smiled—a strange, sweet smile. "Now who would bring messages except The Messenger?" He sort of said it in capitals. I wasn't brave enough to ask any more. I went back to the class. Then it was midday and time to go. I belted off home as fast as I could over the slithery roads.

When I reached the house I flung my bike in one of the stables where it lived and went straight in the kitchen with the message in my hand. Mrs. Korngold was making bread. She looked up, glowering, fathoms deep in one of her fits of misery. Lottie and Zach were standing by watching in a subdued way. I suppose they'd wrangled Mum into letting them miss school again. Not much catch when Mrs. Korngold was feeling low. Thump, thump, thump; she was fairly bashing the dough. I stood behind her and read out the "telegram."

"What? WHAT?" She grabbed me with her doughy hands—all over my duffle coat—then saw the bit of paper. After that it was where did I get it, read it again, etc. etc. Then, when it finally sank in, she sort of rocketed from cosmic gloom to ferocious glee, and after that she started to weep, all happy and sad mixed up. One minute she was crying, the next all radiant smiles, just like one of those mixed-up days you get in March—hail, rain, storm and sunshine, and all on the violent side: like a glacier melting and taking half the landscape with it or something.

"Lottie, Zach," she cried. "I'm happy, my darlings! Happy!"

I got the ouzo out of the cupboard. (Ho ho! I thought—it had gone down to half—but I didn't say anything.) She grabbed me again and whirled me round the kitchen.

"When? When does it say?" She'd only read it four times by this.

"Tomorrow or next day."

"She's coming! My daughter's coming! She's coming back to me!" She wiped away her tears with the back of her hand and did a wild dance round the kitchen table. "Now! Now I'll drink the ouzo."

About half an hour later Dad came in for his lunch. He was beaming all over his face. "You won't believe it," he said, "but the wind's changed. It's gone right round to the south. Wait till I tell your mother—and look, the sun's coming out!"

9

IN THEORY Lottie and Zach should have buzzed off to school that afternoon, what with the day improving so dramatically, but Mum said they could be villains for once and just play outside if they liked. It was marvelous to get out and not freeze to death. There were more bursts of sunlight and the sky showed blue in places: it really was smashing when the sun caught the snow.

"Hey," said Zach. "I wonder what it's like in the wood?"

And that reminded me of what I had intended to do that afternoon, and I must say, it was a brilliant day for exploring. I told the other two my plan and Lottie said she'd come with me, but Zach didn't want to, so he stayed at home making things out of snow and playing about with his sledge by the edge of the lake.

I suppose, if you think of it, exploring and getting lost are pretty much the same thing, but of course that didn't occur to us at the start.

"Gosh! What do you think this place is?" said Lottie, all red in the face and out of breath. We had passed right through the part of the gardens we knew, and climbed straight on up the hillside. We didn't bother with paths, we just clambered our way up through the wood, from one terrace to the next, hauling ourselves along with hand-holds on branches or tufts of grass. Only now we'd suddenly got clear of the trees and had come out on a big white expanse covered with rabbit tracks. We went and stood in the middle, and when we looked back the way we had come we found we could see right over the bushes and trees we had climbed up through. We could see for miles over a vast snowy landscape. There was even a town or two smoking in the distance. But to either side of the garden, and nearer to us, there was only moor. I bet there's not many places in England where you can't see a TV aerial or an electric pylon or something modern. But the moor seemed outside all that—sort of timeless. Like the sea, I suppose. But the sea is always moving about. The moor was still; very, very still. I decided that I liked moors: they were restful.

"This is a lawn," I said, getting back to the job in hand. "I'll make a diagram of it." I'd brought a drawing pad and pencil.

"Perhaps he gave garden parties here," said Lottie. "You know— Earl Bloggs. Look, there's all rose bushes round the edges."

Of course, the plants were all straggly and without leaves, though here and there a frozen half-opened bud hung on.

I said "Would you like just one white rose out of this garden, Beauty? Watch out! I'm the Beast." I shoved my pad in my pocket and started chasing her, and she ran screaming across the lawn into a thick belt of rhododendrons on the far side. She'd found a path, and for a minute I lost her. The bushes here were about nine feet high: it was a spooky little path, somehow. I caught up with her on the far side of the bushes and we found ourselves in another open space, paved this time, and enclosed by a tall hedge.

"Eek!" cried Lottie. "I don't like her very much." She was looking up at a statue on a pedestal. There were other statues too, set all round at regular intervals. I suppose they were meant to be white, but they looked dingy against the snowy bushes.

"What are they?" asked Lottie.

There was a lady with a bow and arrow, and a dog at her feet, and a gigantic bearded man with a bent stick in his hand—lightning?—and one with a trident, and some more ladies in draperies.

"They're Greek gods and nymphs and all that, I think," I said.

"Ugh," said Lottie, "they're horrible. They've got fingers and toes broken off."

The thing I didn't like about them was the way they were all smiling (except for the bloke with the lightning—he had a frown). They might be missing fingers or a nose, but there was this smile on their faces still, a great wide smile, almost a grin. You have never seen anything so sinister as those grinning whitey-gray faces.

Then I noticed a statue of a young man eating a bunch of grapes. He had two little lions and a leopard at his feet.

"Hey, look, Lottie," I said. "I've found your lions."

She came and started pushing the snow off them with her finger.

"Careful," I said. "If you touch them they'll come alive." She jumped back. Then she said: "If you turn your back on them they'll get you."

I'd just started drawing again when she sprang on me from behind.

"You rotten little string bean!"

Another narrow path led off between bushes opposite the one we had just come in by. Lottie dived into it shrieking, and I went roaring after her.

This time the path wound on for what seemed like a long way. Then Lottie found a side-turning: I followed her. Then there were more turnings, but no open spaces. The paths weren't badly overgrown, but they were cold and deep and dank, and after a bit the bushes—still rhododendrons or laurels, something with smooth glossy leaves anyway—began to feel overpowering. Lottie let me catch up with her.

"I wonder what happened to Earl Bloggs in the end," she said. "I bet he came in these gardens one day and he never got out."

"Oh, get on," I said—then suddenly she stopped dead again, and I cannoned into her.

We'd come to a little lawn at last, not very big. There was a man standing in the middle of it, with his back to us, looking down at something. He was wearing an old-fashioned overcoat and a scarf, and he had a tweed hat in his hand. He didn't seem to have heard us.

Lottie said in a loud whisper: "It's the ghost of Earl Bloggs."

"Shush!"

He started to turn round, and just as he did so I got the most weird icy trickle up my spine. I could have stunned Lottie for putting the idea of ghosts in my mind.

The man who turned round might have stepped out of the picture in the ballroom—tall, dark-faced, grim, his black hair touched with gray. His eyes too had the same chill look, and yet there was something about them … they were more vivid than in the picture; they were the same color of blue as Mrs. Korngold's. And he was real; he'd left footprints. But the chief thing I noticed about him in those first few seconds, overriding my fright even, was that he was angry—with a raging overpowering anger. He was glaring in fury—at nothing. Not at us, he hardly seemed to see us: his whole mind was miles away, and focused nastily on someone else.

It wasn't just me he had rattled. Lottie had caught hold of my hand and I could tell from the way she held on she was frightened. I don't know if you've ever had a panic-strickenten-year-old mashing up your bones, but if you have you'll know what I mean. She got behind me, and I think the movement drew his attention.

He put on his hat.

Immediately I could see the thing he had been looking at—another of those bally statues—this one was a dog with three heads. But this is what was wrong—I could see it *through* him. Right through him! I could see it quite plain, the three heads raised and separate and the jaws wide open, as if it was baying. I think it was meant to be a fountain.

He put out a transparent hand towards me. Cold air flowed from his finger-tips … I felt myself going dizzy. Then this strong Northern voice said, "I do beg your pardon. I forgot for the moment." He took the hat off and I could no longer see the statue. Everything had gone solid again.

Still holding Lottie by the hand, I dragged her with me back down the path. It was as if my legs had a life of their own—good old legs, I thought, daftly, get me out of this. We raced away, anywhere, up paths, down paths, any way that would get us back to the big lawn.

I don't know if you've ever tried to get lost, just for fun, to see what it feels like. Lottie and I once tried, where we lived before, but we couldn't do it, we always knew exactly where we were and exactly how to get back. Well, now we knew how it felt. We just couldn't find our way out of the alleyways of bushes. We took this turning and that, till we were gasping for breath. Then we found ourselves back at the stone dog again, but the man had gone.

The second time we landed back at the three-headed dog, I realized where we were, and why the paths led nowhere: perhaps you've guessed? Good old William Blodgett—the bloke with mazes on the brain. That's where we were, in a maze, a huge, vase rhododendron maze—and the light was just beginning to fade from the sky.

"I bet it's the same as the ones at the house," I said. "You know, on the hall floor and that one on the ceiling. It's bound to be. All we have to do it remember the pattern."

"It feels different when it's all looming up all round you," wailed Lottie. "I could prick my finger and drip blood, so we don't go the same way twice."

"Don't be silly. Let me think."

"Well, hurry up then, my feet are freezing."

"I know! It's easy! We've only got to find our footprints where we came in."

All the same, it was trickier than I thought, because by now we'd trampled pretty thoroughly all round the central area.

"Look," said Lottie rather shakily. "That man went out this way."

His footprints were larger than ours. They led out from the center. I didn't notice any leading in.

"Perhaps this is the right way, then."

I can't say I felt enthusiastic about following him, but we didn't seem to have much choice. It worked. After a few turnings we picked up our own first set of steps into the maze. His led over them, but we didn't see him.

We followed our tracks not only out of the maze but all the way across the big lawn and back down the hillside. We weren't getting lost again, no fear!

As we slithered down we got jolly wet. The snow was beginning to fall off the branches and all our footprints had gone splodgy. We could even hear a few birds singing, and sometimes there were tinkling sounds as icicles snapped off.

Once we got through the railings and out of the grounds it seemed lighter. The sun was setting; level beams shone in our eyes—the first clear sunset we'd seen for ages. There was a mild wind in our faces too. We cheered up a lot.

Lottie, of course, hadn't quite seen what I'd seen—the man going transparent, I mean; because I was between him and her. But when we got in sight of our house I couldn't keep it to myself any longer. I told her, and I told her about the potholer turning up at school that morning too.

"Who do you think he is, him and that one we've just seen?" she said in a low voice when I'd finished. *"What are they?"*

"It's obvious, isn't it—they're the same as Mrs. Korngold. But they're getting nastier."

"Well, I'm telling Dad," said Lottie, beginning to sound hysterical.

"Agreed," I said. "No question. Hey, look! What's Zach doing?" We started to run.

From the first the lake had fascinated Zach, and once it was frozen over Mum had to keep him off it. He couldn't skate, but he made slides, and sometimes took a sledge on it. He'd got his sledge out on it now, but everywhere round us we could see snow sliding off trees, icicles melting.

"It'll take a while for the ice to thaw," I said. "But I don't think he should risk it. Zach!"

We both yelled, but he was already twenty yards out when we reached the edge.

"Come back."

"No."

"It's melting."

I stood on the ice. It creaked.

"I heard it give," shrieked Lottie. "Zach! Get off there this minute."

"Why should I? Look at him!"

A man was standing far out, where the lake was deep. It was the man we had seen in the wood. I'm sure it was him, though he was against the sun and you couldn't see his face.

"See," shouted Zach. "That man's a lot heavier than me. Do you want to see my slide? I'm just having one last go."

He turned his back on us.

"Stop!" A girl's voice rang out from the shore. I don't know where she came from, but she wasn't alone. Our potholer was with her, in his woolly jumper, boots, rope over the shoulder and overalls. She was dressed the same, only under the woolly cap long black silken hair hung down.

"It's not safe, Zach," she called, not quite so urgently now because he had stopped when she said to. "Come on, back to your brother and sister."

He came, meek as a lamb, and no harm done. We fussed over him, clipped him round the head for a minute or two, and so on, and when we remembered to look out over the ice the man in the overcoat had gone. Perhaps he just put on his hat again.

The girl was saying goodbye to her friend too, then she came over to us on her own.

"I'm Mrs. Korngold's daughter," she said. "You can call me Cora."

"Gosh! Will she be glad to see you!"—that was Lottie. We left the sledge and rushed in round the back of the house.

What a meeting!—laughing, crying, kissing. I thought Mrs. Korngold was going to eat her.

There was a strong smell of aniseed in the kitchen, and the ouzo bottle was empty. "Now tell me, my darling," said Mrs. Korngold at last. "I want to know everything. What was it like? Then she looked at us and said: "But you're all damp, Lottie. Go and get into dry clothes." And we realized they wanted to be on their own and we faded out into the passage. Zach remembered the sledge and went out to get it.

"Put it away in the shed," I called, and he said he would. Lottie and I went to hang up our coats in the hot cupboard. Then we heard the lock turn in the front door and rushed downstairs again.

"Oh, Dad!" We threw ourselves at him. "You've got to listen to us …" We started gabbling it all out, about the man in the wood, and Cora and everything.

"Not now." He disentangled himself gently. "I'm glad about Mrs.

Korngold and her daughter, and you be nice to them both, but you can tell me the rest later."

"But …"

"Later. I'm just a bit worried about your mother. She was running a temperature again this afternoon. I'm not sure she's not getting pneumonia." He went past us up the stairs.

We sat on the bottom step. Lottie put her arm round me. "Never mind—it'll keep a bit longer. Zach's all right and we are. It isn't as if he fell in, with his ear and everything."

"He wasn't likely to fall in without it," I said crossly, and chucking her arm back.

"Also," said Lottie, "Mrs. Korngold's happy now, so I don't think much harm can come to us."

We sat in silence for a bit.

"And Mum's sick and Dad's worried." It was all right for her: she hadn't actually seen through the man, just heard about it. I tell you, I was still pretty shaken, especially with all that emotion in the kitchen on top of everything. I was glad just to go on sitting there.

Then Lottie said with a sigh: "I wonder what's going to happen next. I don't suppose they're both going to stay here. I bet Mrs. Korngold goes soon. It'll be different when she's gone." Blow me down, she was starting to snivel.

"You really think she'll go?"

"Mm?" sniff. "Of course she will. I think she's only been waiting for her daughter." Sniff sniff.

"O.K., sis," I said. "We'll take the heat off till she's gone, but you needn't think I'm keeping this bottled up for ever."

More sniffs.

"Cheer up, kid—you'll still have Timothy."

Dad came down, stepped over us, and rang for the doctor. He went back upstairs. "Someone'll break their neck over you two," he said. "The wretched electricity's gone again."

Then Zach wandered in from the back somewhere. "What are you sitting here for? Hey, do you know what? There's an owl sitting on our gatepost. I thought it was a statue at first."

"Don't," I said. "We've had enough statues for one day."

"Come and look."

Something brushed against the small pane of glass at the top of the front door.

"No need," said Lottie. "It's here."

She was right. The owl seemed to have gone mad—it kept dashing and dashing against the window, as if it was trying to get in.

I suppose it was some time after supper when the car came. It was quite dark anyway, because I remember we'd lit the candles, being without power.

We had all gone in to talk to Mum—only not too loud—but she wanted to hear about Cora, what she looked like, what Mrs. Korngold said, and so on. Suddenly we heard the roar of a noisy car engine. Then silence. We all listened. We heard a car door slam. Then a ring at the bell. Zach ran down and opened the front door—he can practically see in the dark—and Lottie and I hung over the banisters. Dad was doing a quick tidy-up of Mum's bed.

"Are you the doctor?" said Zach.

"I have been called that—the doctor that cures everything."

"What a funny thing to say," whispered Lottie. "I didn't know there were any doctors like that."

Zach was saying cheerfully, "I thought all doctors couldcure everything."

The man laughed: "There's only one doctor can do that."

His answer gave me that sick feeling you get when a lift goes down too fast. I grabbed Lottie by the arm. "Listen, Lottie—that voice."

The strong North country tones vibrated all round the hall.

"Wha-what's he doing here?" Lottie was mincing up my hand again. Calls himself a doctor? *He's* not seeing our mother, I thought.

But that wasn't what he wanted.

"I'm looking for Mrs. Korngold," he said. "Could you find her for me? My name's Underwood."

"Will you come this way, please. Mind the step." Zach led him off in the dark.

"What are we going to do?" squeaked Lottie.

"I don't know. We'll decide when Zach comes back."

But he didn't come back, so we went down. Very uncomfortable it was, with Lottie holding me by a great handful of jumper at the back. We edged cautiously along the passage. We could hear voices speaking quietly in the kitchen, and before we opened the door Mrs. Korngold called out "It's all right, children, you can come in."

They were sitting at the kitchen table, Mrs. Korngold at the head, Cora in the middle facing us, and Mr. Underwood, taller than the other two, at the foot. The meal had been tidied away and the table was scrubbed and bare, except for a bowl of apples near Mrs. Korngold. Mr. Underwood had put his scarf and hat on the back of the chair. Zach was standing by the fire with his mouth open watching them. We shuffled round behind them to join him, and when we got on the other side of Mr. Underwood we could see what Zach was gaping at—Mr. Underwood had the little owl on his wrist, like a falcon.

"Mr. Underwood is my brother," said Mrs. Korngold. Her hands were clasped in front of her and her knuckles were showing. "He's not staying."

"We've met already," said Mr. Underwood, "in the wood: and I'm not going just yet." He let the owl hop from his wrist on to the table. "We've something to discuss with you, my owl and I." He smiled. His mood of the afternoon had quite changed; he wasn't at all angry any more. The tension was all in Mrs. Korngold. Cora looked pale and tense too. Suddenly she stretched out her hand to take an apple, and the owl let out a screech and fluttered his feathers, making us jump. Cora drew her hand back quickly.

Mr. Underwood said in a nasty smiling sort of way "Take something. You must be famished, not eating anything for so long."

"Squawk," said the owl. "Squawk, squawk." He turned his head through 90° and looked as pleased as an owl can look.

Then Mrs. Korngold spoke in a dull, sad sort of voice. "Your fingers are red, Cora. I saw them."

"I ate some wild strawberries," said Cora, looking down at the table. "Only a few—two or three."

"Ha!" Mr. Underwood slammed the table and gave a triumphant yell.

"Oh, Cora!" Mrs. Korngold let out a groan: then turned on her brother, her face distorted with rage and her eyes blazing. "So that's why you came! You knew! Your spy—that carrion—told you!"

"Hoot," said the owl. His master grinned sardonically. Then suddenly, violently, Mr. Underwood sprang up, shot out a long arm and seized Cora: "She's mine! She's mine!"

"No!" Mrs. Korngold grabbed hold of her daughter on the other side. "No! You shan't have her back!"

Things held still for a moment. We daren't breathe. I saw Mrs. Korngold as I did on the night of the storm, human size but at the same time huge—a vast immovable object, which he attacked with irresistible force. Whatever Mrs. Korngold was, Mr. Underwood was her equal, perhaps more than equal. Will clashed with will. My instinct was to throw myself flat on my face. My brother and sister stood motionless … there was something funny about the way Zach was staring … and Lottie too; she had a queer glassy-eyed look. They were both asleep, open-eyed and standing up.

I went on staring.

I knew who they were. I knew who Mrs. Korngold was. At least, I knew what the Romans called her, and the Greeks—and *before that?* My brain reeled: it was like the night I got loose in time. I felt as if a gong was sounding in my head, and I knew I couldn't stand much more of it.

A peal of thunder reverberated over the house.

"Mine for eight months," cried Mrs. Korngold desperately.

At once a second crash rang out and lightning dazzled.

Mr. Underwood's face changed from triumph to fury. The silence was electric. Then his shoulders sagged. "Mine for four," he ground out.

The thunder cracked a third time.

"There!" shouted Mrs. Korngold, as if she had won, and I suppose she had—a limited victory.

Slowly Mr. Underwood released Cora, and Mrs. Korngold got her arm round her.

Then all the lights came on; Zach and Lottie started out of their trance, and we were all blinking our eyes in the sudden glare, especially the owl.

"This isn't the end of it," snorted Mr. Underwood. He snatched up his scarf and hat. "Come on, Ascalaphos"—the owl hopped back on to his wrist.

"Show him out, Zach," said Mrs. Korngold. "Go on, go together, children."

We trooped out: Zach, Mr. Underwood and his owl, then me, then Lottie. It was brightly lit now in the hall, and the outside light was on too. Zach opened the front door.

Mr. Underwood put on his hat.

I could see Zach right through him—it was just like before. I could feel my hair stir on the back of my head. Lottie, peeping out behind me, went rigid. Zach turned round to Mr. Underwood and found he was looking at me. His blue eyes nearly popped out of his head. Then he was knocked to one side, and this wraith-like figure went down the steps. The gate clicked. He got in the car. It was long and rakish and black, an open sports car, which we'd seen a long time before. The engine roared, the tires squealed, and he went.

We didn't speak for a long time after he'd gone. We didn't even shut the front door. Lottie was shivering, and Zach's knees actually knocked together—I heard them. We sank down on the bottom stair, keeping very close together. We must have sat there for ages, till the fright began to wear off a bit.

"I'm telling Dad," I said. "And this time he'd just better listen."

"Yeah," said Zach. "He'd better."

10

Mum WAS SITTING up in bed drinking a glass of wine, and not looking too sick, and Dad had Beth on his knee, well wrapped up. We just blurted out everything at them.

They heard us out to the end. Then Dad said, "Well, I don't know—it all sounds pretty daft to me. Look, I know you've had a fright, or frightened yourselves. And a few strange things have happened, but if we look them in the eye …"

"They won't go away," said Mum, "Because, if you ask me, there's been far more than a few strange things, and I'm going downstairs now to straighten them out." She got out of bed and put on her dressing-gown. Dad thrust Beth at me, and there was a lot of protesting, with Mum saying "I'd rather do it alone," and Dad saying she mustn't, etc. etc., till finally Mum said, "Please. After all—she's my home help. I know I can manage. Come on, don't look so miserable. Go down to the sitting-room and stoke up the fire—I won't be long."

So we did what she said and just waited, and Dad got a good blaze going downstairs, and we drew the curtains and made it look homely and nice.

"Listen," said Dad after a bit. "Is that fire crackling or is it raining?" Lottie went to look. "It's raining. Gosh! It's pouring."

Not long after that Mum came back. She stood in the door and said with a perfectly expressionless face: "There's another of them there—an old woman: she appears to be Mrs. Korngold's mother." We drank this in in a stunned silence. Mum went on. "Mrs. Korngold and Cora will be gone by morning. The old lady's persuaded Mrs. Korngold to go home. They all seem to have come to some agreement. Cora's going to stay with her mother for eight or nine months, and with her uncle for the rest of the year."

I saw her meet Dad's eyes. He shook his head. Honestly, we mightn't learn Latin and Greek and all that, but we're not that dumb. Just to show—it was Zach who first said straight out what we were all thinking.

"It's like that story we had at school," he said. "Thingy—Phosphorus or Telephone or somebody."

For a minute nobody spoke. Then Mum said automatically, "You mean Persephone. Demeter and Persephone."

"Yes, that's the one," said Zach.

"I don't know what you're talking about," said Lottie.

"Yes you do," said Zach. "There's this girl picking flowers in a meadow. All of a sudden the ground opens and a chariot with four big black horses comes galloping up out of it. It's the king of the underworld, and he grabs the girl and drags her off. Then her mother comes looking for her but she can't find her anywhere. I think he had a cap of darkness, or something; it made him invisible … What happens next, Mum?"

Mum looked doubtfully across at Dad.

He just shrugged. "Why not?" he said. "Go on; tell it."

So Mum went on, in a queer flat voice: "The mother was called Demeter: she caused the crops to grow and the corn to ripen. Her daughter's name was Persephone, only sometimes her mother called her Koré—it means 'the maiden.' Hades stole Persephone, like Zach said, and took her down to the underworld to be his queen and rule with him over the dead.

"Demeter went looking for her daughter everywhere but she couldn't find her. She stopped caring about making things grow. The vegetation died and famine began to spread over the earth.

"At last, tired out with searching, she came to a countrified little palace not much grander than a farm in a place near Athens called Eleusis. The mistress of the house had just given birth to a baby, and Demeter stayed and helped mind the baby. Then she happened to hear how one of the older children had seen Hades's chariot disappearing into a hole in the ground, and from that she guessed what happened to Persephone.

"All this time the land continued to decay. Zeus, king of the gods, sent his messenger, Iris, to bring Demeter back to her home on Olympus, but she refused to return till her daughter was restored to her. The famine grew worse. Zeus sent other gods and goddesses to persuade her, but still she wouldn't go back. She was even happy sometimes with the family at Eleusis—there was just one nasty little boy there, but she changed him into a lizard. At last Zeus sent Hermes with a message. Hermes—you may know him better as Mercury—told Demeter that Hades had promised to release Persephone, provided that she had eaten nothing while she was in the underworld.

"Mother and daughter, full of happiness, met at Eleusis. At first it seemed as if everything had come right—but then a gardener who had seen Persephone eat something whispered to Hades what he had seen. In a fit of rage Demeter turned the gardener, who was called Ascalaphos, into an owl. But in the end she agreed to let Persephone live with Hades for part of every year and come back to her in the spring. Then Demeter's own mother, Rhea, came to persuade her, and Demeter was satisfied, and returned to Olympus, the home of the deathless gods."

After that there was a long silence.

"Do you think that's why the winter was so bad?" I asked at last.

Dad said quickly, "We've often had bad winters. It was winter, now it's spring. Let's just hang on to that."

But of course we couldn't. "I wonder why she didn't stay up at the Hall? That's more like a palace than this is," said Zach.

"For some inexplicable reason," said Dad, "she seems to like children."

"I like Mrs. Korngold," said Lottie, starting to get het up again. "I don't want her to go."

"We like her too, love," said Mum, "and yes, you do want her to go, really."

Mum was right. It was grand and marvelous—but more than we wanted.

"In the story at our school," said Zach, "it was pomegranate seeds she ate. What does a pomegranate look like?"

Dad said: "We had them a lot when I was a boy. They're round and hard and a bit like a lemon on the inside, but dark red and full of seeds. It's the seeds you eat; you pick them out with a pin."

Mum said: "Pomegranates, strawberries—it doesn't matter as long as they're red. Red is the color of food in ... well ... Hades." She knows a lot of stuff like that.

"Like the blood out of the liver," I said.

"What was that?" said Dad. "No—don't tell me now. When they've gone ... let's leave it till then."

"Mrs. Korngold wants to say goodbye to you," said Mum. "You, Adam, and Zach and Lottie. Don't be afraid—she only wants to be nice to you."

"Do you think they'll be all right with her?" said Dad, holding Lottie back.

"Yes, yes. They'll be all right. Anyway, there's no point in drawing back now; we're all in it—up to the neck. There's nothing we can do but trust them."

We went down to the kitchen. They were wearing their outdoor clothes, and Mrs. Korngold—I still thought of her as that—was putting a few things in the old black bag she had when she arrived. We didn't see the old lady properly—just a glimpse of a long dark skirt as the back door slowly closed on her. I was glad of that. Mrs. Korngold looked up when we came in, with a happy expression on her face, not overflowing with joy like she had been before, but pretty contented. Perhaps for our sakes, she'd sort of diminished in some way. I don't mean in actual size—she still looked large and strong—it's hard to explain—she just looked calm and mild again, so we weren't frightened.

"Just getting ready to leave," she said cheerfully, "with my daughter."

"Your daughter doesn't look like you," said Zach.

They both laughed. "No," said Mrs. Korngold. "Well—we just borrow a shape. Sometimes I'm fair, sometimes I'm dark—whatever takes my fancy."

"See?" said Lottie to me. "He did look like Earl Bloggs—your brother, I mean, Mr. Underwood," she added more politely. "He must have borrowed William Thing's shape."

I don't know why she was going on about it—I wasn't arguing. Actually, I was thinking about Mr. Swift.

"Oh, *he's* always doing it: he loves changing shape," said Cora, "he can't resist amusing himself." I hadn't uttered a word about him, but I expect she was like her mother, and could look into your mind.

I don't know whose shape she had—she was like one of those dancers, they're ballerinas, I think—the pale beautiful faces and smooth hair—Lottie's got some in a book. Gosh, she was pretty. I suppose I was staring.

"I think you should leave us now," she said gently. "And as you've all been very nice to my mother, in the morning you'll find there are nice surprises for you—presents. Something you'll like."

"Goodbye, children," said Mrs. Korngold.

"Goodbye," we said. We didn't dare to touch her. We just went out and closed the door.

I suppose it was a bit of an anticlimax, but I had some geography homework to do, so I went upstairs and did it. Actually I didn't get it all done, because Mum had suggested an early night for all of us. So I left it, had a bath and went to bed.

I slept all right that night, except that once or twice I woke up and heard the rain. All night long there were slooshings and runnings and soft sploshes as the snow fell off the roof in chunks. I don't know if you've ever seen (or heard) a really good thaw. It was very relaxing. I lay there listening and wondering just a little bit what sort of presents we were going to get in the morning. I wondered if Mrs. Korngold would know what we really wanted. For some reason I thought they'd be made of gold …

Came the dawn—and Zach with it, rubbing his ear and saying did no one hear the alarm, and how it had gone right through his head.

"Shush," I said, because about thirty seconds before he woke me—it felt like that, anyway—I had had this remarkable dream, and I wanted to fix it. I'd dreamt of Mrs. Korngold again. This time there was a moon shining, and I was in a street somewhere and looking up at it over the tops of houses. Mrs. Korngold's face appeared in the sky. She was sideways on to me and dazzlingly beautiful, sort of shining and golden. She started to turn her head towards me and I felt pleased. But when she did, on the other side she had the face of a horrible old woman! Ugh. Actually, I didn't think I would forget it.

I threw on a few clothes. I'd thought of how to finish my homework, too, so I quickly scribbled a few sentences, and then we went to find Lottie.

She was in the kitchen, just walking around, picking things up and putting them down again. The kitchen was clean and tidy, and empty. Lottie had a sort of smug look on her face, but she didn't say why.

"They've gone all right," said Zach, opening the pantry door to make sure. "I wonder when they went. I wonder if they got wet."

Lottie still seemed to be mighty quiet. "Are you all right?" I asked. She heaved a sigh.

"I was wondering which one Cora wanted to be with, really," she said. "Didn't you feel a bit sorry for Mr. Underwood?"

Honestly, girls. "Oh, *you*," I said. "I bet you feel sorry for Hitler because he lost the war."

"Well, I just wondered, that's all."

"Come on, daftie," said Zach. "Let's tell Mum and Dad they've gone."

We dashed upstairs. As we burst in, Dad was saying, "I believe you're better! Your temperature's gone."

"Sure!" said Mum. "I feel great."

"They've gone," said Zach.

Dad said that was as it should be.

Mum told us to hop off. "I'm getting up," she said.

"Do you think that's sensible, Diademia? I mean …"

"Aw, quit worrying, honey, I'm fine." She beamed round at all of us—"Really fine. As a matter of fact, I haven't felt as well as this since before Beth was born. Do you know—I think I'll ring the Pembertons and ask them over for a glass of sherry before lunch."

"She's better," said Dad. "Push off, kids, while we get dressed."

"I know—I'll say we're celebrating the change in the weather," said Mum. "That's a good British thing to celebrate!"

We filed out.

Two minutes later the door was flung back on its hinges.

"Don't talk to me, anyone," Dad said. "I've had an idea and I want to try it out." He'd thrown some clothes on all anyhow, and went hurrying down.

Mum ran out to the head of the stairs. "Your jersey's on back to front! Oh, never mind"—he was already struggling into his overcoat. "Do you want me not to bother with the Pembertons?"

"No, it's all right. I'll be clear by lunch. I'll ask them—I'll be seeing Sir Charles. You needn't ring them. Where are my gloves? …"

"Will you remember?"

"What? Oh yes, of course I'll remember." He opened the front door. "What a nice day. I don't need my gloves. Goodbye."

"David! You haven't had any breakfast!"

"What? Oh. Yes. No. Breakfast?" He sounded as though he had never heard the word before. "Never mind," and he was gone.

Mum said, "Exit the mathematician. I'll ring the Pembertons."

I wonder if you've spotted it about the presents? I was wrong to think we'd get something made out of gold: but what about Zach hearing better? You could count that as a present, couldn't you? I mean—he can even hear bats squeaking, now—that's a very high note, in case you didn't know: most grown-ups can't hear it. Also: Mum got her health back, and Dad got his equation to converge! Whatever that means. Anyway, he came back from the lab after a couple of hours, grinning from ear to ear. He'd put his sum, the one he'd had going for weeks—about his underground explosions—through the computer, and it came out the way he wanted it to. Pretty ordinary gifts in a way, perhaps—the sort of things that were in us already maybe—only brightened up a bit. I mean, Zach wasn't ever really *deaf*—it was just that his range was limited, he used to have trouble with low tones and high tones, only not any more. I'm not too clear about Beth: she doesn't cry much, but then she never has. There's one thing for sure—she's a very blooming baby.

Would you like to hear about Lottie's present? Well, Dad had calmed down a bit and called a quick meeting in the sitting-room, to make sure none of us said anything peculiar in front of the Pembertons, whom he *had* remembered to ask for drinks at twelve. Unusually for her Lottie was gazing into the mirror over the fireplace.

"Hey, look at her," said Zach.

"You're not supposed to stand on the kerb," I said. "You better get off. Mum's coming."

"I gaze into the mirror," said Lottie dreamily, "the mists swirl away, they part ... What do I see? I see a beautiful young lady. She is stunning—adorable ..."

"Can you really see her?" asked Zach.

"No, not really." She got down quickly as Mum and Dad came in, but she still had that "cat that got the cream" look.

Again, in a way it was quite ordinary: all that had happened was that she had found that old photograph of Aunt Cecilia when she was a little girl. You remember? The one I told you about that had got mislaid. And Mum was right—Aunt Cecilia, when young, might have been Lottie's twin, the nose, the hair, even the braces on the teeth—and we all knew how she'd turned out: a looker—soppy brown eyes and all.

"Where did you find it, honey?" Mum asked her.

"It fell out of an old book of hers: in that lot she sent for my birthday. She had it when she was growing up, and I was reading it in bed this morning."

"What's it called?" I said.

"'The Care and Management of the Pony.'"

"Mon dew," I said. "Wouldn't you know?"

"Mother," she went on, "I'd like you to call me Charlotte, not Lottie. You know, like Aunt Cecilia is always Cecilia and not just Celia."

"Well, all right, honey. We'll try. We'll all try—" glaring at Zach and me. "Meet your sister, Charlotte."

"Dad," continued our sister, Charlotte, "where did Aunt Cecilia go to college? Do you know what she was good at at school?"

"Holy Moses," said my father. "Not another child psychiatrist in the family."

"I don't want to be a child psy—what you said, but I wouldn't mind being a doctor—or a vet." She looked hopefully at Mum.

"All right, Lott-er-Charlotte: you can decide later."

Well I think there was a present in all that somewhere.

Mum said, "Now about Zach's hearing: you'd better know, our doctor in Kent always said he might just naturally improve." Her voice tailed off, and I may say as far as we children were concerned she just found herself looking from one disbelieving smile to another.

"Well," she said defiantly, "that's my story and I'm sticking to it."

"Your mother's right," said Dad, after a moment's thought. "It's the only way to handle it. We know what we know—but who's going to believe us? Imagine your aunt getting her hands on a story like this—"corporate family hallucination," or some such nonsense she'd call it. We'd be in the papers! And me, a serious scientist!"

"A joint family hallucination?" said Mum. "Mm. I wonder …"

"Perhaps that's what it was," said Dad. "I'm beginning not to believe it already."

"No!" said Mum. "I can't shrug it off so easily. I shall remember Lottie coming off Timothy till my dying day. And where did Mrs. Korngold get her back from, I'd like to know? Not that I actually suspected anything queer at the time."

"When did you?" Lottie asked.

"On your birthday," Mum said. "You remember those gorgeous peaches Mrs. Korngold gave you? I'd seen them when they first came into the house, all shrivelled and dried up. I wondered why she'd bought them. Well, you saw what she did to them."

We all fell silent, recalling this and that, I suppose. A thought struck me.

"I bet she goes and stays with someone every year," I said, "and people never notice. Well, some people wouldn't."

Dad wasn't impressed. "Maybe," he said, bestirring himself. "We'll go into it all in more detail this afternoon when we're on our own, but this is our plan for now: *it never happened.* That's how it's got to be. Just talk about ordinary things while the Pembertons are here, and say nothing."

"Right," said Mum. "Now come on, you can all help me. There's still some tidying up to do."

Funnily enough, the work was quite a relief. We found we were glad to be straightening ordinary cushions on ordinary chairs, dusting our ordinary table, etc., and getting ready, as we thought, for a bit of ordinary hospitality. Like Mum said, you can only stand so much grandeur.

About ten minutes later we hear their car.

"We felt lazy," said Lady Pemberton, "so we drove. But it's such a beautiful day we should have walked. Hallo, children."

"We were wondering," said Sir Charles, when he had got out of the car, "why we couldn't see the lake from the house. It surely must have been intended to form part of the view. What do you think?"

"Perhaps it's just that trees have grown up here and there in between and spoiled the original plan," said Dad.

"Maybe. And of course—we can't see the house from here either."

"There is one place you can see the house, Dad," I said. "Just round by the end of the lake. I usually look out for it on my way home from school."

"Shall we take a little stroll and see?" said Dad.

"What about a drink first?" said Mum, just out of politeness.

"Let's go and look while we have our coats on," said Sir Charles.

"I'm rather interested in this—I've got quite fond of old Blodgett and his plans. Pity his son didn't care for the place."

It was sunny and mild, and the birds were singing. We didn't even bother with outdoor clothes. We all strolled along happily chatting. A narrow dirt road ran all round the lake: it was quite clear of snow now, just a bit damp still.

"This is the place," I said. We were all standing in a little grove of saplings through which you could quite plainly see the Winter Palace. "Sometimes I could see the sunset reflected in the windows," I said, "when there was a sunset."

I got a jab in the ribs from Mum at that point, but Lady Pemberton only said "Yes, dreadful winter, wasn't it. Really shocking. Seems to be over now, though … Good heavens! What is it? What's happening?"

There was a grinding, roaring sound, like a million bags of coal falling, and the ground rippled towards us. It was like a wave of the sea, but it stopped before it reached us. A full-grown tree at the left-hand end of the house tipped over sideways, quite slowly at first, then faster, till it crashed. At the same time, the building cracked open up the middle. Like the tree, it started to topple. It was so weird and slow, it made you think of a large heavy person doing a sideways bend at keep-fit. William Blodgett must have gone all lopsided in his picture in the ballroom. Chimneypots, urns, pillars, made arcs in the air—clear as anything against a pale blue sky. Seconds later, the whole end of the house fell down. Great clouds of dust arose and hung over it.

I can't remember how long it took us to get over the shock. Dad and Sir Charles went rushing up there, and the police came and the fire brigade and so on and so forth. Luckily, no one got hurt. The house had tipped over into a deep gash in the ground. It ran right up the hill behind the house, too, into the wild garden—as far as the maze, I bet, but we haven't been allowed to go and look.

Actually the end where the Pembertons lived was left standing, so they were able to get their furniture out. Some of the scientific equipment was saved too, including the computer, but the building's no longer safe. Demolition men are going to blow it up when the investigations are over.

A day or two after it happened Dad came whistling in at the garden gate—we were messing about outside—and said "Guess what—we're moving, my chickens. The Ministry doesn't like this place any more. It doesn't want its valuable scientists disappearing down any holes. They're going to dismantle the labs and shift them."

Lottie was the first one to send up a wail, closely followed by Zach and me.

"The pony! "

"The lake!"

"My room!"

"We'll find somewhere just as good—don't worry."

"I bet we don't," said Zach.

"Dad, you don't think … it had anything to do with Mrs. Korngold? The ground giving way, I mean?" I asked. (It was what Lottie, Zach and I thought. We thought Mr. Underwood had done it in a fit of temper.)

"You've been wondering about it, have you?" said Dad. "I know—it's not easy to forget, any of it. But … come in the house. I've thought of something we can do. Adam, get your mother; we'll have a family council on this …"

Well, that's more or less where we came in. As you know, we had our conference and I got stuck with this writing job. While I've been doing it the family has been getting ready for the move—to Warwickshire, that's a bit south of here.

I've almost got to the end now. It's extraordinary how friendly I feel towards you-in-the-future, telling you all this. I just hope you're going to think more of it than my family do. I'll tell you what they said when they'd had a look at it.

I tottered into the living-room with a great pile of manuscript, i.e. hand-written—you'll have gathered that what you've been reading is Dad's typescript.

"Gosh, what a lot of writing!" said Zach admiringly.

"You've finished it?" said Mum. "You mean you've really finished it? David—come and look!"

I don't know what was so amazing about it. The way they went on you'd think I'd never finished anything in my life before.

Of course, things changed a bit when they actually read it. I would have thought they'd be proud of someone with almost total recall, wouldn't you?

Dad read it first. As he was reading he was saying things like I used "sort of" too often, and "colledge" hadn't got a D in it, and there was no 'f' in prophetic and what awful scribble, didn't they teach me punctuation, and stuff like that. Then he said: "It's a very *detailed* account. Did you have to put in all those *details*?"

I said: "But, Dad, it was you who said boys my age don't know what's important and what isn't, so they tell it all."

"That's right, honey," said mother, "you should always tell it how it was."

(She didn't say that when she read it.)

Anyway when he'd finished Dad said it wasn't quite what he expected but perhaps it wasn't all that bad, and he was pleased with me for completing such a long piece of work, and that he would type it out with proper spelling in and more full stops, but not changing anything. He didn't, either, only where I'd told about looking out over the landscape that stormy night, and seeing mile after mile under the lightning, where it said "the three-fanged mountain", Dad had penciled "Tryfan" with a question mark in the margin. That's a mountain in Wales. I'd really like to see if it was that. And where I'd put that bit about Mrs. Korngold saying "fish and guests stink after three days," he'd written: saying used by Romans (see Horace).

When it was typed Mum read it. She sort of exploded and said she always knew boys were gabbier than girls and that this was the most scatterbrained piece of writing she had ever read, and I was supposed to be accurate about Mrs. Korngold, not about her chucking teapots and sugar bowls about, and making it sound as if she *drank* all the time. (Actually, she doesn't.)

Then Lottie read it and said it was mean to give her away about eating the chocolate cake at the Pembertons the night Beth was born, and that if Mrs. Korngold ever got to read what I'd said about the ouzo she'd turn me into a frog or something. Also, why hadn't I put in about her learning to ride Timothy, and how good he was now? But she didn't care about Gregory Dawson saying she looked like a stick insect, because she knew she didn't, so there. That was a good thing, because I'd forgotten I'd put that bit in. This thing has taken me so long to write I found I'd forgotten quite a lot of what I'd put in at the start, and I'd left out some things I'd meant to put in.

Zach hasn't read it at all, because he's been too busy making another airplane out of plasticine.

Of course, I shan't ever know what you think about it. (By the way, I'm typing this section out myself, so it's quite private, between you and me. Also there won't be much of it.)

The house has gone now—about three weeks ago they finished it off. Zach was the sorriest about it—he always liked it, but do you know, I was quite glad. I wanted something to be different after all that has happened. There's no doubt though—it's made an awful gap in the landscape. We keep going out to look at where it isn't, if you see what I mean, and Dad comes with us and says things like "Things fall apart, the center cannot hold"—that's another poem we've never heard any more bits of.

I expect you've guessed: it was subsidence that caused the house to collapse. Apparently there were very deep tunnels right under it. Part of the wild garden did fall in too—the whole of the maze, the statues, and the three-headed dog. The Ministry of Power naturally said it was due to old mine workings, but that's not what Zach, Lottie, and I think. We think now it was *one of those places where you can enter the underworld*. Well, they had them all over the place in Greece and Italy at one time, according to Mum. We think William Blodgett just happened to build his house over one of them, only we reckon it's blocked for good now.

I expect the wilder parts will really take over: I suppose I really hope they will. I liked the wild garden—with those plants from the Himalayas that have gone native. I wonder if they've got waves of energy rippling through them all the time—like when I looked out of our study window with Mrs. Korngold back in the autumn.

By the way, you remember that town where we got the Green Shield Stamp present? Dad says there's some talk about their Council buying Blodgett Hall grounds for a Country Park … that would let the local people back in again—the ones whose ancestors were shifted by Earl Bloggs.

Well, we're going now. We've said our goodbyes to this Stately Park of England (in the case of some of us "goodbye Stately gardens, Stately lake, Stately grass" etc. etc. Our sister Charlotte hasn't changed all that much), and we've packed the car. The last thing Dad and I will do before we leave is to bury this—good and deep, but not too deep for you to find one day, I hope. Then we'll get in the car and go.

I must tell you this: just now there was a ring at the door. Lottie and I ran down. There was a man in overalls on the doorstep. We froze.

"I've come from the electricity board," he said.

Oh yes, I thought, which one of them is this? I sort of goggled at him and said: "Oh … er … please, won't you come in?"

"Yes, please come in. You're very welcome." Lottie sounded more nervous than me.

"I've only come to read the meter," he said—and that's all he seems to be, a man to read the meter.

The Institute found us a place in a new block of flats. I bet strange things happen in blocks of flats, too—though you don't feel as if they're going to. I bet in your time blocks of flats are like quaint old country cottages are to us … Anyway, we didn't take it, because there was Timothy to consider. You're not going to believe this— we're going to live in an old windmill. There's no lake, but there's a little stream, and Zach and I were wondering if we could widen it and dam it to make a pool, so there'll be plenty to do.

So long then, and good luck.

And remember my deep thought that Mrs. Korngold (though under some other name, I bet) comes back somewhere every year and doesn't get spotted. Don't forget us going out to look at the space where the house had been and still getting a shock every time, because that just shows you how hard it is to take in anything out of the ordinary.

So watch out—you never know, it may be your turn next.

> Your friend,
> *Adam Bramble*
> Adam Bramble

P.S. Hey! I've just thought of something. Did you notice I was the only one who didn't get anything from Mrs. Korngold? You don't think *finishing things* was my present, do you? *Mon dew, sapristi* and *parbleu!*

Honestly. Some present!

AFTERWORD

In the early 1980s, before my first novel was published, I got a job at Harold Ober Associates, one of the oldest literary agencies in the United States. A perk of the job was the chance to read from Ober's well-stocked shelves of books written by authors the agency represented. One of those books was *The Gods in Winter*, by Patricia Miles.

As I began to read, Adam Bramble's clear, straightforward boy's voice caught me up. I lived with quietly astounding events as the great goddess calling herself Mrs. Korngold takes charge of the Bramble family one strange winter, fixing their meals as she provides miracles, dusting rooms as she grants their children visions, helping with the new baby as her fellow gods come to beg her for the return of summer. The story set hooks in me, drawing me deep into it. Intent on the pages as Adam laid out each new detail, I felt awe as the ancient story of the kidnapping of Persephone unfolded in a modern British home.

I left Ober for office jobs, then full-time work as a writer. I read hundreds, probably thousands, of other books for adults and children. Some of the books were very powerful, and most were thicker than *The Gods in Winter*. And yet I could not forget Mrs. Korngold, solid in her kitchen, smiling slightly as she caught the annoying Bramble cousin in cake theft. I couldn't forget the mazes in floors, ceilings, and gardens, or Adam's vision of the entire world that night when Mrs. Korngold put her hand on his head. I wanted to read the book again, to see if the story was still as powerful as I remembered it, but I couldn't find it in bookstores or libraries.

I mentioned *The Gods in Winter* to librarians, to editors, and to my agent at Ober. It was my agent who finally sent the book to me—and then he began his own quest, to see if someone would be interested in publishing it again. Fortunately for me—and, I hope, for you—he found someone at Front Street. That's why you can read this book for yourselves.

I re-read *The Gods in Winter* the moment I took it out of the envelope. I wasn't mistaken. The story still gives me the shivery feeling of captivation that it gave me the first time I read it. I've had that same feeling on every reading since the book came back into my hands. A novel like this, one that grips my imagination, when I have read so many books—I think it will grip you, too. I think you will understand the hold of Mrs. Korngold's flinty smile, the wonder of three schoolchildren who witness the affairs of the gods, and the power of an ancient story unfolding before you. You won't see your own everyday kitchen the same way again.

—*Tamora Pierce*

PATRICIA MILES was born in 1930 in Lancashire, England. After graduating from Oxford University's Somerville College, where she studied Latin, Greek, and ancient history, she lived with her husband in Rome for a year before they settled down in the house where she still lives, in Hertfordshire, near London. Her first children's novel, *Nobody's Child,* was published in 1975.